S P A R K

Tracy Blom

and

Jimmy DiResta

Copyright © 2020 by Tracy Blom

CONTENTS

CHAPTER 1

The Ace of Swords

Ben slowed his motorcycle, nearing the signs of an accident that held a whisper of death in its wake. A fiery red Porsche had lost an argument with a highway sign that told drivers only twenty miles stood between them and downtown. As he drove past, the vacant blue eyes of the dark-haired driver slumped over the wheel held the promise of more to come. For far too long, guys like that have lived recklessly in the shadows of wealth. But a new day was coming.

The light of the Harvest Moon illuminated the country road as he sped towards the city, lost in a thought he had been chasing for days. He had set some things in motion and no amount of regret, second-guessing, or whirlwind of law enforcement would put a halt to those efforts. He would make them pay for what they'd done.

The criminal masterminds behind the infamous Chicago Tylenol, Sudafed and Oronamin C murders produced dozens of copycats. None of them reached the level to which Ben aspired. Those were hit or miss, while his plan had everything to do with the things that some people couldn't live without. The panic, fear, and uncertainty would gain the attention of everyone who mattered, and would make sure the world knew exactly what they had done. After all, the only way to put out an oil fire is with an even bigger explosion.

He hugged the corners of the road, nearing his destination, thinking back to a simpler time, before reforms in the packaging of over-the-counter substances and federal anti-tampering laws. He, in his zeal to make sure justice was served, had found a way around even those.

The red brick building came into view. The place, which provided work to nearly seventy-five percent of the people who lived in the town of East Durham, brought home the reminder of his role in the problem. He worked for one of the largest cigarette manufacturers in the country, feeding addictions one paycheck at a time.

Day after day, his efforts amounted to soulless work for the almighty dollar. One might compare it to the detached slaughterhouse worker, knowing that life is being taken, yet food had to make it to everyone's table. Even his own.

"Hi Ben," a raspy, familiar voice called from behind while patting him on the back.

"Hey Linda." He watched her hobble past him, taking an elongated drag of her cigarette before flicking it into the bushes near the entrance. The slight limp was compliments of an accident that happened on a night she shouldn't have driven home from the local bar, but even that didn't keep her from having a good share of the town's men grace her bed on those rare lonely nights.

"Anything new going on?" Ben asked.

"Put mustard on my bologna sandwich instead of mayonnaise," she quipped. "Other than that, same old, same old."

"Sounds about right," he said, taking in the fact that she had eaten the same thing for lunch every day for nearly fifteen years.

Linda was what Ben referred to as a "lifer" at Zamka Tobacco, someone who had worked at the plant since she was old enough to earn a paycheck, and would continue on until some version of the job killed her. Sometimes he pitied her. Her husband had left with a younger woman a decade ago, the moment he lucked into an inheritance, deepening the lines of sadness already worn into her face. Other times, Ben wondered why she didn't just figure out what she wanted in life and go after it—anywhere but here.

Ben paused at the door to grab the thermos from his old canvas bag as Emelia walked in.

"Evening, boss man," a voice with a huskier promise snapped him to attention. "You bring me something good in that container?"

"Coffee and cream," he said, with a smile.

"Nah, you can keep that cream," she crinkled her nose in disgust. "I'm not trying to spend my shift paying respects to the porcelain goddess."

Ben chuckled, then his gaze narrowed, following Emelia's line of sight as a darkness came over her expression.

The floor, brightly lit by lamps that hummed a static tune, was busy with an odd hybrid of people and robots, a sampling of automation that the higher-ups had been testing. Everyone had mixed feelings about the new "electronic" additions to the unhappy family; except for those whose jobs they had already displaced.

Emelia's husband had been one of those people. Now he spent his days scouring the want ads, which meant Emelia took on extra shifts to make ends meet and put three kids through college. Her weariness showed in the depth of her eyes, but a little hope existed there, too.

Ben's extensive background in farming tobacco, coupled with his scientific accolades, had ensured his job security. At least he liked to think so. He had the operations of the plant down to a science, unlike most people who came in, punched a card, and walked out to their version of the American nuclear family. Ben had studied every part of the organization meticulously. Working the graveyard shift was by his own design. During the wee hours of the night was when he could look under the hood of the machine and tweak it as he saw fit.

Everyday ran like clockwork. At 12:01, he parked his bike. At 12:05, Linda arrived with her signature bologna sandwich before spending the next five minutes running back to her car for things she had forgotten. Ben would spend the next two hours walking the floor and monitoring the additives applied to the sheet tobacco.

Over seven thousand additives existed in the cigarette world, and each one brought its own unique property to the final product. Some prolonged the shelf life while others simply masked the harshness of the nicotine. The robots oversaw this part of the process and allowed the perfect scapegoat for what was to come.

At two in the morning, Linda stepped out for her third smoke break while he tipped over to her station to check her work for errors, which he found more often than he would like. After he secretly rectified her mistakes enough that she wouldn't lose her job, he stepped out the back door and walked through the woods to the second warehouse. The long gravel drive and seclusion of trees reminded him of the acres of land where his farmhouse had been built. But his land held far more secrets than these woods could ever bear.

The warehouse is where he spent the next two hours examining lamina- the whole tobacco leaf, blade, and stem- checking for quality and recording his findings. Something about the aging process intrigued him. Maybe it was how the same plant could change drastically just by being exposed to a few different variables.

Between four and five he returned to the main building and ate lunch, which typically consisted of a delicious culinary experiment put together by his wife.

Right around 5 a.m. he heads towards the opposite end of the building where research and development takes place. The next hour was his favorite, and provided complete unmonitored, uninterrupted solitude before the interns arrive.

For the next two hours he attended resident lab studies and instructed young ambitious students on the bio molecular effects of cigarettes. This was his least favorite part of the day, as it reminded him of what happens when addiction swallows the mind.

"That's enough for today." He snatched up his belongings and hurried out through the swinging door, nearly knocking a student in the face.

"Wait, Mr. Flowers," Andi said, her voice breathy and sweet as she smoothed her dark, silky hair behind her shoulders. "I mailed out that package for you. Is there *anything* else I can do for you?"

She looked doe eyed and thirsty. Too thirsty for a man of his age to take a drink.

"Not today, Andi."

"Well," she said, playing with the edges of the cleavage baring blouse which caught half of his attention. "How about tomorrow?"

He paused, working his way around what that slight offering meant. "You know what? I'd like to show you something if you have a moment."

Andi's dark brown eyes widened to the size of saucers, the innocence in them almost made him give in to their promise. Almost. "Of course."

She stayed tight on his heels as they walked through the warehouse, hurried down a set of stairs and entered a secluded section of the factory at the other end of the building. He reached for the keys that dangled at his hip, checked for bystanders, then slid into the private lab. As the door closed behind them, he could feel her excitement brimming. She had been waiting so long for Ben to notice her, and finally he had.

A single wooden table stood in the center of the bright white room, lined with shelves of beakers, microscopes, and a myriad of foreign instruments. Cameras pointing down from the corners all focused on the same object—a tall cabinet in the back of the room.

"I have to admit I was shocked to see you enlisted in this program," he said as he walked further into the room. "With a background in computer sciences and near perfect GPA, your talents seem somewhat wasted here. Last year you won the Kleene Award for an outstanding paper on computer science theory, and now you're interning at a tobacco company?"

She parted her thin pink lips to protest, but he held up a hand to ward off anything she had to say.

"But the more I watch you, the more I understand why you're here. You're one of the brightest students in this program. You know that, don't you?"

Andi adjusted her glasses, giving him a bashful smile. "Well, I—"

"Which is why I'm going to let you in on a little secret, but you can't tell the others okay?" He snapped a fresh pair of gloves on his hands.

She nodded as he unlocked a tall cabinet in the back, revealing a hidden room. Silently, she followed him in, her gaze sweeping the walls of colorful test tubes. She attempted to look away from the cages of lab rats sitting on the counter, instead focusing on the other more favorable items.

"For the last few years, we've been working on developing a new line of cigarettes which have images that appear on the paper when lit. These special cigarettes require specific additives and correct ratios of heat sensitive ink. To create something like this takes a highly skilled, steady-handed, scientist." Ben shifted his gaze so it locked on her. "This is where I think you can help. As long as you don't mind coming in a little early one day a week?" He reached for a single glass bottle on the highest shelf.

"No problem at all," she replied, scanning the far reaches of the lab as though committing every inch to memory. Her gaze returned to the squealing cages, as she asked, "what's with the rats?"

He continued pulling bottles from the shelf, preparing for the demonstration. "Every hypothesis needs to be tested. Now, if there are no further questions I'd like to proceed?"

She nodded in accord.

"I can show you how to make the first one, and after that you'll be on your own."

She watched in excitement as he zipped around the room like a mad scientist, grabbing dyes, papers, tobacco, and needles. As he carefully dotted the paper with heat sensitive ink, a set of numbers slowly came to life. He paused, looking up from his creation.

"Oh, now Andi, this is very important so listen up. The numbers that go on the cigarettes have to match *exactly* what is written in this binder. Corporate wants to turn this into some kind of treasure hunt game, so the numbers cannot stray from what is written here," he warned while tapping the binder.

She blinked several times as though sensing something was wrong in the process, but couldn't exactly pinpoint it enough to ask the right questions.

"I understand."

"Now, watch where I put things back so that you remember."

He returned the objects to their rightful places before sliding the newly created cigarette into a manilla envelope alongside a note. "You wouldn't mind dropping this package off for me on your way out, would you?" He heaved an oversized box onto the counter and taped the envelope to the top.

She couldn't decipher if she was an appreciated scientist or glorified errand runner, but accepted the task regardless. "Sure."

"I hate to ask any more of you, but there is one more thing," he said, moving closer to the point that she inched backward. "You're pretty good with computers, aren't you?"

"Mmm hmm."

"Do you think you could help me with my cell phone? I bought cameras for the warehouse and don't quite know how to see them on this thing." He fumbled a little as he extracted the phone from his pocket. "And please, don't tell anyone ..." He leaned in as though there were more people in the space besides the two of them. "But Linda ... she used to have a drinking problem. The other day, I saw her take a bottle of something and slip it in her purse. I keep a lot of powerful substances in here and I'd just really feel better if I could see what was going on at all times."

Andi grinned as he placed the cellphone and a set of keys in her hand. "That shouldn't be too hard."

"Stay in here as long as you need to, and when you're done just leave my phone on the table."

She raised a curious eyebrow. "Wait, don't you need your phone?"

He paused in the doorway. "I'll be just fine without it. I prefer the old landline anyway."

CHAPTER 2

Two of Wands

Late night fog rolled through the pine trees as a man with frazzled hair, a slight beer belly, and handlebar mustache emerged from his house tucked deep within the forest. The sound of distant waves called from the shoreline as he walked in silence towards an unmarked package waiting for him at the end of the drive. "Great, more instructions," Tom Wilson grumbled while removing the envelope taped to the top of the box. Inside of the envelope was a loose cigarette and a cryptic note that read, 'Saturday's haul, executive suite, this box only. I'll be watching."

Since the age of seventeen Tom had been delivering goods. What started off as simple food delivery quickly evolved into a C-class license and long days on the open road completing hauls for big brands. People in small towns have big dreams, and Tom was no exception. He had found the perfect opportunity to spend his days nearly unsupervised, running packages, named or not, for whichever vendor paid the most. Monday and Tuesday were devoted to the seafood industry, running fresh fish from the harbor. Wednesday through Friday he spent hauling goods for the plastic company; one day to pick up, one day to drop off, and one day to drive back. Saturday was devoted to Zamka Tobacco, distributing cigarettes to the good folks of East Durham, and even stocking the vending machines at their corporate headquarters. While he had access to many things at Zamka Tobacco, he certainly didn't have access to their executive suite.

Squinting, he studied the side of the loose cigarette, questioning his vision. He rolled it between his fingers trying to make out the faded numbers that appeared beneath the paper, then carefully tucked it into the pocket of his flannel shirt.

He opened the front door, and called up the stairs, "Hey, sis. I'm heading ..." He paused, remembering he no longer had anyone to answer to, then walked room to room turning off the lights, treating each switch like a memory. Even after all these years he could still hear her nag, "I wish you didn't do hauls at night," but there were some jobs he preferred to do in the privacy of the shadows, and this was one of them. She was what he referred to as superstitious, but the truth of it was, she was in tune with the universe at a level he couldn't fully comprehend. Certainly, she would have objected to him fulfilling a job during Mercury retrograde, a time she swore evoked errors and misfortune.

He clutched the keys in the palm of his hand, grabbed a pack of matches, and headed for the door with the new package wedged tightly beneath his arm. He had always planned out his hauls ahead of time, ensuring proper delivery of everyday packages along with a few high-paying others.

The edge of the forest disappeared behind him as he drove in pensive silence towards the city. A lot was riding on getting this particular package to the right place, more than he cared to think about. He glanced to the passenger seat, eyeing the mysterious box that had somehow become his highest paying job, thinking of only one thing, his sister. Life had dealt her a hand of cards she should have never looked at, and now she spent her days locked away in the nicest care facility money could buy. A place he never would have been able to afford without jobs like this one.

As the silhouettes of buildings emerged through the haze blanketing the city, he dipped into his memories of her, pulling out a painful one. He could still see her tear-soaked face looking back at him through the window of the bolted door. She was locked in a prison of misunderstanding, and those she loved the most had put her there.

On the brink of town was an isolated loading dock, a once secluded place that now was cluttered with a growing population of homeless people. He pulled in, put the truck in park, and turned to make sure no one sneaked up and caught him unaware. Seeing no sign of impeding strangers, he hopped out, package in hand, and walked to the back of the truck.

Okay Tom, set the package down for just a second, open the door and wait for the haulers. He could feel the sweat beading up on his forehead as he looked around for the typical team of workers. Just as he set the package down a loud bang came from the front of the truck. He crept slowly around the side, attempting to see who or what had caused the noise, only to find a drunken kid whose outfit looked as if he had escaped the circus.

"Sir ... sorry to bother you, mister trucker man," the homeless man slurred while belligerently waving an old top hat in the air. "Will you give me just a few bucks? I could really use something to eat."

"Sorry, not right now." He scanned the lot, seeing only the two of them.

Where were those haulers? They should have been here by now.

"Ricky. The name is Ricky."

"Whatever," Tom snapped, shifting focus back to the job at hand, which at the moment, was lying unattended on the ground. He hurried to the back of the truck, but halted at the sight of a red-haired thief whose arms were stacked with boxes.

"Drop those boxes or I'll shoot!" Tom fumbled for his pistol that seemed to be missing as the thief in the top hat yelled, "Run!"

The two men disappeared into the maze of shipping containers, dropping boxes as they fled. Tom turned back to the packages scattered upon the ground, frowning at the identical boxes. He had taken such pains to properly arrange them, and suddenly they all looked the same. *Which one was it?* Damn thieves may have just cost him this job and any hope for future assignments. He couldn't call anyone to verify, and this package had to be delivered tonight or else he could kiss the money goodbye.

Tom checked the first few packages trying to see if there were any tell-tale signs that it was the one he had received earlier, and selected the box closest to him. Silhouettes of shadows rounded the corner as the haulers finally emerged onto the scene. One of the men paused near the back of the truck, eyeing the scattered boxes on the ground.

"Everything okay here?"

Clearly, they hadn't seen the robbery. No need to tell them about it now. That would only stir up questions. "Slipped from the skid," he winced as the lie slid from his lips.

They checked the truck contents, initialed his paperwork, and left him standing alone with only a hope that he hadn't made a terrible mistake.

His phone vibrated as he checked the incoming text. "Train station, locker seven. Smoke for code." Lucky for Tom, East Durham was one of the few small towns left in the country that still maintained public lockers in train stations. It made for an easy exchange of money with no questions asked.

* * *

Tom hurried his pace, weaving between the static of people, aiming to reach the designated locker. He pulled the cigarette from the pocket of his shirt, lit it, and stared in awe as a code began to appear on the paper. His hurried fingers turned the dial, revealing a duffle bag, half full of his promised pay, a key card to the executive suite, and another note that read: finish the job and you'll get the rest.

* * *

Jake yanked the back of Ricky's jacket, keeping him from falling into the street. "Look at you. You're a mess."

Ricky hiccupped. "So, we got it didn't we?" he staggered into the near empty road and headed towards the train station. "Wait, what did we get?"

Jake opened his jacket flashing a few treasures from their find. "Four cartons of smokes. Was hoping for something I could give to the kids, but hey, we still have time left in the day." Jake gestured towards the concrete stairs of the subway. "Come on. Let's get down there."

Ricky's greasy fingers slid across the subway tiles as the two boys submerged into the tunnels to their usual spot. Dollars piled into the old hat as Jake captivated one person after the next, leaving the credit cards for Ricky and the cash for himself. They had perfected this scam to a science.

Jake scanned the crowd, bypassing a woman who had probably seen better days on the other side of fifty, and homed in on the designer-clad cloud of perfume stepping off the train.

"Care to see a magic trick?" Jake flashed his once dashing smile as she turned up her nose. He took a swing at her ego, "You're probably too old to appreciate magic anyway."

She flinched, hugging her blue Birkin bag to her breasts like a pillow. "I'll watch your trick, or whatever it is."

Jackpot! "Okay, I'm going to shuffle these cards here, and all you have to do is tell me when to stop."

She casually stroked her long black hair, her expression bored and unamused. "Okay, stop."

"Jake ..." Ricky attempted a failed whisper.

"Not now," Jake scolded between clenched teeth, keeping his focus on their latest prey. Someone carrying a Birkin had some dollars to toss away. "Okay now, pick a card, look at it, and put it back."

As the woman played along, Ricky interrupted once more, "Jake, there's that same guy, over at the lockers... you know, the trucker. Look, he just pulled out a duffle bag... could be money." He flailed his arms, knocking a credit card loose that didn't bear either one of their names.

"Thief!" she screamed as they scrambled for their things. That one damning word alerted a nearby cop who wasn't close enough to nab them if they managed to sprint in the opposite direction. For a split second, Jake caught the eye of the trucker, who should have screamed a similar word, but instead seemed just as spooked as he was.

"Run." Jake swiped the card off the ground and swooped up his scarf full of items as Ricky pushed his way through the crowd. They fled through crisscrossed alleyways, separately making their way towards the meeting spot several blocks away, where Ricky sat catching his breath behind the donut dumpster.

"That was freaking nuts." Ricky laughed between ill-mannered chews that nearly turned Jake's stomach.

"You think that's funny?" Jake pushed him backwards. "You almost got us caught."

"Ow." He rubbed his chest. "Sorry. I swear, there was a man in the train station doing something really shady."

"Like we weren't?" Jake shot back.

"This was different," he protested, still glancing over their shoulders as though that portly cop could have finally caught up with them. Possible only because they were stationed near a donut shop and the cop had wanted his nightly fix. "All I'm saying is that he wasn't there to catch a train. I think he was picking up money."

"Speaking of." Jake reached into his coat pulling out a handful of plastic options. "Let's go pick up stuff for the other kids. I'll get the food; you pick up clothes and blankets. Meet back at the church in an hour."

CHAPTER 3

The Magician

—•◦•◦•—

The light of the morning sun rolled across the city, highlighting the two boys drinking coffee on the steps outside of Zamka Tobacco's corporate office. With yesterday's earnings nearly spent and distributed, they were eager to get a start on the day. The early risers began to trickle in, flooding the sidewalks with the essence of money, reinvigorating Jake's pleading. The eye rolls and dismissals seemed a tad different today, and suddenly he realized why.

"Hey, we forgot to change." Jake nodded towards their clean new clothes. "Hurry, hand me my bag." Jake slid on an old hoodie and removed his new shoes while Ricky combed his dirty hands through his long dark hair, ensuring he still looked the part. He adjusted a tattered shirt over his lanky frame and placed his old leather top hat on the ground between them.

"Put that away too." Jake said while nodding towards his cell phone.

"Sir ... sir... one minute, real quick," he rasped. "I know you're in a hurry, but if you could just spare a little change. We're trying to get a room for the night." Ricky scanned the man with the lost blue eyes who wore the familiar trappings of a designer suit and tie. The CEO of the company, whose steps they often defiled, was his favorite as he always said exactly what was on his mind that day, usually consisting of blows to their manhood mixed with some variation of disgust. Today he seemed busier than normal, not even stopping to give the typical "fuck off" or "get a job", before disappearing into a corporate tower that housed everything from fine dining to Pilates. Today, he whispered frantic words into his cell phone as he raced into the glass and stone building.

"See that, he rolled his eyes." Ricky chuckled, always happy to get a rise from this particular man who reminded him of his dad from the times when they used to speak. Back then, Ricky had hopes and dreams that would take him as far away from East Durham that the Greyhound could manage.

Jake shrugged, pulling a smoke from the half-empty pack in his jacket. "Wonder what's wrong. Think his wife is stepping out on him again?" He laid back on the marble steps and exhaled a cloud to the sky as people rushed around them.

"Ma'am? Any change?" Ricky called to the woman wearing a pair of black stilettos stopping long enough to stomp out a cigarette beside him. She didn't bother to respond. Each dismissal varied from person to person. Most acted as if they simply didn't see or hear them, while others made up hurried excuses. Truth of things, they were happy living on the streets—free entertainment, free shelter when they wanted it, and free time.

"Sir, spare any change? We're so hungry."

An uptight man with a shiny bald head and seasoned tweed suit picked up the pace.

"Come on," Jake taunted. "Let's go to that new diner. I've been wanting to check it out."

The bald man, still within earshot, wrinkled his face in disgust as he spat, "Unbelievable."

"Oh, you did hear me." Ricky spun around, walking backwards as he stared at a group of pencil skirts—women who looked empowered and strong, yet somehow scary.

"Watch where you're going, junkie." Hot coffee spilled onto the sidewalk as a polished lawyer-type threw his arms up in the air.

Their laughter echoed through garbage-filled alleyways as they headed past the back doors of businesses and made their way towards the popular diner nestled between a record store and a florist.

"Watch this lady's face when I ask for a table," Ricky said as he pressed his dirty hands to the glass door.

On cue, her porcelain face soured as she said, "Can I help you?"

He smiled, baring the yellows of his teeth in all of their unwashed glory. "Table for two."

She paused before snapping two menus from the podium and guiding them to a table as far away from other patrons as space—and inhalation—would allow. "This place is for *paying* customers..."

"How much for eggs and bacon?" Ricky asked. "Oh, and coffee. Two coffees."

She scowled. "Six bucks for eggs and bacon, and two dollars for a cup of coffee."

Jake rifled through his pockets, dropping loose change as he unwrinkled a few dollars. "Looks like ..." He did a mental count and added, "Yep, we'll have one order of that."

"Wonderful," she mumbled, tossing the menus onto the table and hurrying off to a group of businessmen who were probably much better tippers.

An odd silence lingered between them as Ricky prodded. "What's the matter?"

Rays of sunlight poured through the window, accenting Jake's crisp blue eyes. "I had another vision." He retracted into silence as the waitress slid plates of bacon and eggs between them.

"Well?" Ricky asked, shoving an entire strip of bacon into his mouth.

"I don't know if I was asleep or awake, but I saw it clear as day. It was like I was flying over the forest and I heard a voice call out from the pine trees, "come find me." I narrowed in on a golden glow coming from within the trees, and saw a lodge of some kind, with big glass windows, balconies, and a woman seated on a bed. She got up, like she could see me, and placed her hand on the window. I mirrored her, placing mine to hers, and as we pulled our hands away the prints were exactly the same."

"What do you think it means?" Ricky said while chewing.

"The woman was my mom...I think, maybe she's still alive."

Ricky laughed, "Meh, I like your other visions better."

Jake scowled. "You mean the ones that provide you with monetary gain?"

As much as Ricky hated the fact that Jake was gifted, he had learned to appreciate it over time, or rather, take advantage of it. Jake's second sight had gotten them out of more problems than he cared to recall, but remained a topic of contention. In Ricky's eyes, it was just another thing that made Jake better than him. After all, Jake had left behind everything Ricky always longed for in life; a family that wasn't terribly broken, and parents who didn't abuse him.

Jake and Ricky polished off their breakfast, even managing to leave a decent tip, before making their way to the subway in time to catch another influx of passengers. Jake handed Ricky one of the last of their shared packs of smokes, a habit they'd picked up during grammar school that escalated to a two pack a day habit by the time they reached the age of sixteen.

People filed on and off that silver transport in chaotic order as Jake laid his scarf upon the train station's pavement, spreading a deck of cards and old dirty items across it. Another one of the ways they made their living on streets that hadn't been too kind to boys like them. Boys that had been thrown away by parents who had more money than sense.

"Who wants to see a magic trick?" Ricky announced like a Las Vegas showman as he raised his leather hat to the sky. "Come one, come all to the greatest show in the subway." Cards spread between Jake's palms as people slowed, watching objects appear and disappear without reason.

"You, yes you, like to see a magic trick?" Jake's smile gleamed at a nearby woman stepping off the train. "It'll only take a minute." Before she could check her watch, he pushed on with his dramatic spiel, "Ma'am, right here. Watch my hands now..." Once he secured her attention, fingers slid across the cards. "Now, I'm going to shuffle these cards, and all you gotta do is tell me when to stop."

As Jake's fingers made a few deft movements, she nervously checked her watch. "Okay, stop."

"Now, take a card and look at it." He nodded towards the deck, ignoring those who had gathered close by to watch, providing just the right amount of cover the duo needed. "Just pull it out and put it back."

He resumed shuffling, as she began pacing a few inches before their setup. "How much longer?" she insisted. "I really have somewhere to be."

Jake stopped, revealing one card in excitement. "Is this your card?"

"No."

"Hmmm, you know what, why don't you check inside your purse..."

The woman quickly peered inside, pulling out the queen of hearts. "This... this was my card. How did you..." Her eyes widened in shock as she tucked her purse to her chest.

"It's magic," he said with jazz hands–a series of finger wiggles that aimed to be expressive and equally as dramatic as his voice had been.

She hurried away as Ricky chuckled. "Try putting it in something else next time. Purses are too predictable."

"Penny for your thoughts..." A towering man held a crisp hundred-dollar bill over his head as he made his way towards them.

"'Fraid I don't know that much." Jake gave a dismissive laugh to hide his nervousness.

"I don't need change," the man said, his voice holding a note of mystery. "Just need to know how you did that."

"Steal?" Jake opened and closed his palm, flashing a stolen credit card and a smile.

"How'd you put that card *inside* of her purse? You never even touched it. I watched you."

Jake continued shuffling. "I told you... magic."

Another train pulled in, bringing more victims for the plucking.

"Hundred dollars if you do it again," he challenged. "Only this time I want you to put it *into* something unopened."

Jake flickered a look at the vast crowd, mentally calculating which would be the best victim. "Anywhere in particular?"

The man jammed a hand in his shopping bag, pulling out flowery tissues and a perfume set. "How about this? I just bought it for my wife."

Ricky gazed into the near empty top hat, thought it over for a split second. "Come on Jake, we could use the money."

Jake rearranged the objects scattered across his scarf, placing the black feather to his left, amulet of crystal to his right, and a pocket watch in front of him.

"What are those for?" the man demanded, suddenly seeming more concerned than he needed to be.

"Helps me concentrate," Jake replied as he picked up the cards. "Now, I'm going to shuffle these cards here and whenever you're ready you just tell me to stop, okay?"

The man watched in pensive apprehension. "Now."

"Pull one card, look at it, and remember what you drew."

He continued shuffling the cards, as the florescent lights of the subway flickered casting an eerie shadow over the platform. The man looked up for half a second as Jake clapped his hands. "Now, check that bag of yours."

The man tossed the flowery paper from the bag, searching the gift set for signs of intrusion. Carefully, he pulled the shiny wrapping from around the gift, laughing as he did. "Guess I'll be rewrapping her gift now."

They waited in silence, as he pulled the lid from the box.

"Well, I'll be damned."

Jake and Ricky stared at the bill, waiting for it to fall from his hands. "So, how'd you do it?" he asked, continuing to study the package.

"Can't tell ya that..." Jake's smile faded as the man pulled back the bill. "Wait a minute... you said if I did the trick again, you'd give a hundred."

"I did, didn't I?" He placed the bill and a business card into the hat. "If you ever want a real job, give me a call," he said before disappearing into the crowd.

Before Ricky could get a handle on things, Jake extracted the card and flicked it onto the train tracks.

"What'd you do that for?" Ricky stared at the tracks wondering if he had time to go after it.

Jake replied, "I don't want a job."

"You didn't even see what the card said." Ricky watched as passengers alighted, and the next ones got on. Jake's focus remained on the pack of cigarettes he'd stolen when the man had his attention elsewhere.

"Didn't need to."

"You could have just turned down the biggest opportunity of your life ..."

Jake struck a match and lit a cigarette, watching as the train sped away. "He'll be back."

CHAPTER 4

Four of Pentacles

⬥ ·✦· ⬥

"About time." Gina whispered, caressing her thigh before inviting Scott Daniels in.

For nearly an hour, she had reapplied layers of lipstick and liner, ensuring she looked as sultry as the last time. On the rickety plastic chair, her designer gym clothes lay folded. After all, that *was* where she said she was going. It provided the perfect excuse for why she returned home every Wednesday night with tangled hair and a flushed face, not like her husband Sam would ever notice.

Outside, the neon lights of the two-star motel buzzed with anticipation as Scott entered, quickly closing the door behind him as though someone might actually recognize them in such an out of the way place. He smiled at the extravagant set up she had clearly brought from home: silk sheets, satin pillows and an array of scented candles. He threw his keys on the counter beside the can of Lysol, knowing she had thoroughly sprayed the bed.

"Can take the girl out of the mansion, but can't take the mansion out of the girl?"

Sensing his playfulness, she sauntered to the bed with an exaggerated sway of her hips ensuring he noticed her new lingerie. She settled among the pillows, slid her fingers between the folds at the apex of her thighs, and gave him an intense glare. "You know me... I enjoy the finer things."

He slipped from his noose of a tie and joined her on the bed. "Sorry I'm late."

She climbed on top of him, grabbing his shoulders like handlebars. "I'm just glad I have you to myself for a few hours."

A thick vibration came from his pocket as she smiled. "Did you bring me a present?"

Scott pulled the phone from his pants and rolled his eyes. "I'm sorry, this will only take a minute." He held up the offending device and stood from the bed.

She rolled over in a huff and closed her eyes, attempting to ignore the conversation which continued to interrupt her slippery fingers in action.

"I told you I had to work late," he insisted. "What? What do you mean you got robbed in the subway? What credit card did they take? Why did you even have that one?" A few moments lingered as he listened, then said, "We'll handle this when I get home" —then a brief pause—"I don't know when... whenever I'm done." His words were reminiscent of phrases Sam often said, which made her wonder if she was making another mistake.

Relief flooded his face as he tucked the phone back in his pocket and dropped his pants to the floor. "Sorry about that...where were we?"

Her eyes remained glued on the oversized mirror at the foot of the bed, examining the situation from another point of view. From here, she looked beautiful, sexy, maybe even worthy of a better man. All the money in the world couldn't fix her existing marriage, and the diamond choker wrapped around her neck was a sore reminder of how she wound up there in the first place. She moved her long blonde hair to the side and tilted her head, admiring the curves of her body as she traced her fingers down her stomach. It had been years since Sam had shown her any form of affection, and there are only so many toys you can try before longing for the real thing. So, while Scott wasn't the man that she wanted, he was the man that she needed, and nearly as wealthy.

"You like to watch huh?" Scott moved into position behind her while taking in their reflection in the mirror.

"It's just that…" She gripped the sheets as he leaned in and slid directly inside. No foreplay. No kisses. Nothing that would invite her own pleasure. Yes, she could definitely be with a better man.

"Just what?" His words were matched by a groan as he went deeper.

"Just…" She pushed away and reached for his tie, pinning him to the bed with his hands above his head. "Just that we said we were leaving our spouses and you're still married." She tied his hands and inched herself over his face waiting for his tongue. At least he was good at that part of things. "Now, I think you owe me." She gripped the headboard, her nectar dripping down the side of his face as another vibration came from his phone.

"You didn't change your mind, did you?" She slid down on the hard reminder of why she allowed his excuses as the phone continued to ring. The insistent ringing sped up her rhythm, as he struggled to formulate thoughts.

"I …" he closed his eyes, savoring the moment before instinctually reaching for his usual post sex cigarette. Finding his hands still tied he looked to her. "Little help here."

She smiled and didn't move an inch. "You didn't finish what you were saying."

"I need a cigarette." He nodded towards his pants where four missed calls flashed upon the screen.

Gina placed the cigarette to his lips, lit it, and paced the room for several minutes, contemplating the best way to voice her frustration. "Why do you do this to me? Every week we come here and every week you say it's almost over... but it's not, is it?"

Silence lingered in the air as she turned to face him, "Well?"

His face had turned a strange shade of alabaster. She gasped, "Oh my God, Scott?"

The cigarette fell to the sheets as she shook his lifeless body. She checked his pulse, performed CPR, started dialing for help, but then put the phone back on the cradle. If Sam found out she had been seeing someone else he would leave her penniless, just like he found her.

The phone vibrated once more as she hurried around the room, throwing on her gym clothes while eying the ghastly form of her tied up lover.

The neon lights flickered as she slammed the door behind her and headed for the parking lot where her Mercedes waited like a white horse. The light of the Hunter's Moon shone in the rearview as she checked her face in the mirror, cheeks flushed with lies, and headed for home.

* * *

The morning sun blared through the rusted windowpanes, highlighting the charred remains tied to the bed with designer pants still on the floor. A wealthy businessman in this part of town, tied up, and burnt to a crisp. No luggage. No personal items. This was a love affair gone wrong, but how?

Luther had been a police officer in East Durham since he turned twenty-five and had worked his way through the ranks to become the Chief of Police. He had seen a lot of things in his day, but never anything as puzzling as this.

He circled the bed, wondering what kind of person could leave him in such a state and not call for help. Or did they? The last time he saw something this upsetting was fifteen years ago when the bodies of six migrant children washed up in the river. All had been poisoned, and not one of them was over the age of twelve.

"Hey Chief, want me to start marking evidence?" a voice called from the doorway, returning his attention to the present.

Luther nodded as Kevin, the newest high-strung rookie on the force, dipped beneath the caution tape and entered the room.

"Oh man." He covered his mouth, attempting to keep his breakfast down. "He had to have done something pretty bad to end up like this, right?"

Luther knelt and examined the pants, removing a cell phone and a wedding ring from the pocket. "Thirty missed calls. What do you want to bet one of these is his wife?" He hated to be the one to tell her that the 'death do us part' had kicked in, and it was during a kinky tryst gone wrong. "Make sure you dust this phone for prints."

"And the Lysol?" Kevin picked up the can as Luther cringed.

"Gloves, Kevin. You've got to remember to wear gloves." He shook his head in disappointment.

"Sorry boss." He returned it to the counter and nodded towards a freshly opened pack of cigarettes on the nightstand. "Hey Luther, want me to tag these too?"

Luther's stare could cut steel as he waited for the newbie to put gloves on.

"Hmmm." Luther leaned in towards the body, plucking the culprit from the bed, then looked back toward the can of Lysol.

"What's that? A cigarette butt?" Kevin extended an evidence bag.

"Mmmm hmm," Luther commented, dropping the item inside. "Look at the position of his arms. Looks to me like he was tied up. Question is, who lit the cigarette? I'm going to go talk to the motel clerk, see if they have any security footage."

He dipped beneath the yellow tape and headed for the parking lot where a bulky camera and microphone waited. He had to hand it to her, Sally Childs was one of only four journalists in East Durham, but never missed a beat when it came to getting a story. Word travels fast in small towns, and Sally made sure to speed that up.

"Luther, I mean Chief, can you tell us anything about what happened?"

He stepped aside, making room for the coroner to pass. "Look, Sally, I know you're just trying to do your job, but this is a murder investigation and there isn't much I can say at this point."

She stepped in line with the doorway, attempting to look over his shoulder. "Was there a fire?" She squinted towards the charred remains and covered her mouth. "Is that the body?"

He angled to block her line of sight and keep the cameraman from getting any footage. "Again, there isn't much that I can tell you at this time. We are attempting to locate security footage from the motel and uncover the identities of those involved. What I can tell you is there is a male that is deceased inside."

She turned off her mic and motioned for the cameraman to leave. "Off the record. This is the second death this week. Is something bigger going on?"

He scoffed. She had a lot of nerve trying to get at him again. "Off the record Sally, I wouldn't tell you if there was."

CHAPTER 5

Five of Chalices

The sun came up as the next shift rolled in, reminding Ben just how much he enjoyed the robots' company. They were never late, always quiet, and devoid of human error and unnecessary addictions.

"You know what's wrong with this thing?" Hal, one of fifteen sales-clones, repeatedly slapped the cigarette dispensary. His oversized belly wobbled with each blow, reminding Ben of a story he had read in a science journal years ago. Rats were administered small doses of nicotine every time they touched a specific bar in the cage. Not only did the rats learn the patterns of reward, but when the nicotine was taken away, they became violent, ramming their bodies against the side of the cage nearly injuring themselves.

Hal slapped the machine once more before abandoning it for the nearby coffee pot. Technically, the sales guys had no reason to be on this floor, but they, too, had learned the patterns of the third shift workers who always had freshly brewed coffee waiting for the caffeine deprived. Another walked in, eager to grab that morning pick up. The pungent odor of his nighttime habits was an offensive mix of cheap whiskey, sweat, and strangers all covered up by Old Spice.

Ben cringed as the man announced himself to the room, "Closing a big one today, boys." He waited half a second for any form of praise or challenge. None was forthcoming as another, more arrogant salesman entered the room.

"Small potatoes compared to what I'm working on." He laughed as he kung-fu kicked the vending machine, knocking loose the stuck cigarettes that Hal failed to obtain.

"That stuff will kill ya." Ben casually looked up from the newspaper the morning shift had left behind, interrupting their garbage banter.

Hal wiped the sweat from his forehead, "Not if my wife doesn't kill me first." He wheezed as he shoveled his morning snack cake into his mouth.

How could someone who cares that little for his own well-being have a wife? Maybe they were similar creatures and she neglected her well-being in much the same way. He watched the man wobble from the room, looking more like a penguin than a man who ran a successful sales team.

He returned his focus to the newspaper as Linda walked in, just in time for him to mouth the question at the same time she asked it out loud, "Anything good?"

The typical response failed him, as he muttered only a sound, "Huh."

"While I'll be darned," she teased, leaning on the counter. "Did the paper finally print something that caught your eye?" She waited five impatient seconds before leaning in to look over his shoulder. "What's that say? Mysterious fires?"

He folded the paper and headed for the door.

"What do ya think caused them?" She dug in her purse for a lighter as they passed the bathrooms and made it to the parking lot. A fresh cigarette clung to her bottom lip as she nodded towards his bike. "It's gonna be winter before long. You can't ride that thing forever. Call me if you need a ride, okay?"

He nodded, though he had no intention of taking her up on the offer. "Thanks Linda."

Ben settled onto the bike, adjusted the mirror, and took off. She was right, it was getting colder by the day. Soon the country roads would be consumed by winter's hunger. He'd continue to ride his bike until the first snow. Well, maybe the second, or third if it wasn't that bad. Hell, he'd rather ride in a foot of that stiff white stuff than ride with Linda again.

The last time he allowed her to give him a ride home from work was just before Christmas. She had polished off a bottle of peppermint schnapps at work and blamed the smell on candy canes. He half believed her. The fact that she managed to attempt that lie meant he would never trust her again.

He chuckled to himself as he slowed down to decide which road he wanted to take home today. Both led to the same place, but he favored the seclusion of the woods over the cornfields.

Ben signaled right, and disappeared into the forest, crossing the first of three bridges. Over time, each one had grown into his psyche. The first, the old covered bridge, made him feel like a superhero, if only for the few seconds, as he sped through the darkness of the tunnel. The second, and perhaps his least favorite, hung between two cliffs lingering over the rushing river. Some strange part of him secretly feared that he would be the demise of it, sending those last rotted planks of wood called a guardrail to their watery grave with one unwarranted acceleration. The third, his favorite, marked exactly one mile to home.

He parked his bike near the barn, then moseyed up the path towards the warm glow of the kitchen where his wife,

Maggie, hovered over the stove, stirring herbs into her favorite stew. Her typical cheery greeting was replaced by stark silence as he walked in the door. Perhaps she hadn't heard him come in. He dropped his bag on the counter, but she remained unmoved.

"Honey, is something the matter?" He placed his hands on her shoulders and she shivered, probably at the coolness that he brought in with him.

Maggie was a lovable woman, shoulder-length brown hair, pale blue eyes, a figure hidden beneath years of good cooking. A once gifted scientist in the field of emerging technologies who had been convinced to leave her work and take on the role of housewife. Her brilliant mind now tasked with creating exceptional stews, handmade sweaters, and tackling a variety of home renovation projects. She had become a cookie cutter mold of a wife, with all the right answers and a sunny disposition about her. Except for today.

"Have you seen the news?" She wiped a tear from her face before it spilled into the soup.

"No ... I, I haven't. What is it?"

"Someone set fire to the McGinnis' house. The entire thing burned to the ground." Her hand shook as she released the ladle and a shiver of alarm went up his spine when she added, "But... it wasn't just the house ... baby inside and everything."

Ben wrapped his arms around her waist looking over her shoulder towards the door. "Where's Tristan? He's going to be devastated."

Tristan had been friends with Kyle McGinnis since the age of five. They had been nearly inseparable until Kyle found a girl at college that slowly stole his time and attention.

"He had class today. Should be here any time now." She rounded the kitchen island, rushed into the living room, and flipped on the television. He was fast on her heels.

Together they watched in silence as the tragic news spanned every local channel. The headlines varied from station to station, each covering a different version of the same story. All with the same horrific outcome.

A reporter planted her fleshy form beside the blackened bones of a wood framed house as firefighters extinguished the last of the flames. She paused, composing herself before speaking. "I'm standing in front of what once was a happy home. What we know at this time is that there were people inside that weren't able to escape the flames. Authorities are working around the clock to pinpoint the cause of these mysterious fires ... wait, one second." She pressed a finger to her ear, blinking rapidly for several moments before she put her focus on the camera again. "I've just been given word that another fire has broken out in a dormitory at the university."

The phone rang, causing them both to jump.

"I'll get it." Ben wound his way into the den, hoping that Tristan hadn't been anywhere near the McGinnis house. He laid the remote on the bookshelf before picking up the receiver. "Hello."

"Ben, this is Sam Stockton," the CEO of Zamka Tobacco said. "I'm sorry to call you at this hour, but we have a matter that requires your expertise. I need you to come to my office tomorrow afternoon, one o'clock. I'll send a car."

"No need to send a car," Ben said, hoping that whatever necessitated his presence wouldn't interfere with his plans. "I'll take the train. See you tomorrow, Sam."

"Ben?" Maggie called from the doorway, concern etched in her round face. "Who was that?"

"Just someone from work."

She always had a good read on him. "Everything okay?"

"I have to go into the city tomorrow afternoon."

Maggie followed behind him, wringing her hands in a way that signaled she was nervous for some reason. "Will you be gone long?"

"I'll be back before sundown."

CHAPTER 6

The Wheel of Fortune

Autumn was Iris' favorite time of year. The bold colors of the leaves inspired frequent lipstick changes, and the crispness of the air allowed for cozy, oversized sweaters. On sunny days she could be found in the park, seated cross-legged on the ground with tarot cards sprawled out on an old paisley printed scarf.

On a day just like this, Ben had first laid eyes on her. He had cowered behind a nearby tree and wondered if the pink streaks running through her bleached blonde hair were a result of the sunlight or some flippant decision she had made since last week. Her façade changed as frequently as the leaves, which crunched beneath his feet as he neared.

"You're in my light," she said to the silhouette overshadowing her scarf. Her tone had been light and playful. As she shuffled the cards, her multi-colored nails painted like a rainbow drew a smile from his stiff lips. He hadn't noticed her freckles from far away, but up close he could make an assessment of her true hair color and nationality.

"Irish?" Ben queried.

"Iris." She set the cards down and reached for a small velvet bag, placing an amulet of crystal between them.

"Well, that's a pretty name."

She raised a shielding hand to her forehead, locking eyes with the man she had only seen in dreams. "Sit," she insisted while patting the ground. "This one is on me."

Something within him cringed at the thought of this... what was it, magic? But he didn't believe in that sort of thing. So, he entertained the blue-eyed beauty. She watched, amused as the stocky man awkwardly attempted to find a comfortable seat.

She smiled. "First time?"

"Huh?" His attention seemed lost on the cards.

"Nothing to be nervous about honey." She leaned in with a serious glare. "Unless you got something to hide?"

Ben sat as attentive as a schoolboy awaiting her instructions.

"Pick up the cards and split the deck, then hold a question in your mind as you shuffle. When you feel like it's time to stop, place the cards upon the scarf."

She pressed her hands into the grass and breathed as if she were inhaling all the earth cared to share about him.

Ben stopped shuffling and asked, "What are you doing?"

"Connecting to the energy of creation." Sensing his hesitation, she continued, "Do you want to know why Fall is my favorite season? Because it reveals the cycles of the universe all in one beautiful act. The roots nourish the tree, which feeds the leaves, which return back to the Earth as they fall, beginning the cycle over again. In this cycle of creation there is a voice that I hear in my stillest moments."

"That's beautiful." Ben resumed shuffling while admiring the tree they sat beneath. No question came to mind. His thoughts were too enthralled with the eclectic beauty before him.

"You're either a hard worker or very lonely." She chuckled while nodding towards his callused hands.

"Farmer," he asserted. "Tobacco."

"I don't typically see farmers here in the city. Which means you either really like this park, or something else brings you here week after week."

"Are you going to do the cards or what?" His cheeks grew warm as he set the cards down.

"Of course, I'm just playing with you." She snatched the cards and began placing them face up on the scarf.

Ben's face wrinkled as he studied the Egyptian pictures, depicting his destiny in three simple cards.

"That's it?" You can tell all you need to know in three cards?"

"The cards are more like a compass that point me in the right direction. The rest of the information I receive differently." She smiled while running her fingers through her platinum hair. "Now, let's look at your first card which signifies the past."

He laughed at the image of the golden phoenix. "You think that weird bird can tell you about my past?"

"It seems your past has been filled with trials and tribulations, hardships ... things that brought you down to nearly nothing. One of the phoenix's greatest gifts is the ability to rise from the ashes and be born anew. From your past, you will find a new part of you that will be ignited by love, a type of love you've never experienced before."

Ben remained silent as she moved to the next card with a bright green background and a single symbol in the center.

"This is the lotus," she said. "An ancient Egyptian flower that symbolizes the balance of both male and female energy.

The water it sits in symbolizes uncovering the depth of your soul, true hidden feelings, and exploring the mysteries of life." She paused and reached for her water bottle to take a sip. "Here, in the present, you are being welcomed to explore life, love, and accept where the universe has led you." Those intense blue eyes locked in on him. "Does that make sense?"

"I've been alone for quite some time. Does that mean the universe wanted me to be here ... with you?"

She smiled. "Let's see what your future holds shall we?" She picked up the final card, depicting an Egyptian goddess surrounded in colors of blue and red with arms raised proudly above her head. "The Savior of Flails symbolizes a great warrior; one who will fight endlessly until victory is won. This person is ruthless, skillful, and victorious. It means that... whatever war you end up fighting, the ends will justify the means. Do you have any questions?"

"Well, I don't like the sound of that. What do you mean by war?"

"Hold on." She closed her eyes as if she were mentally going out to retrieve the answer and would be right back. She exhaled, "Okay, so, what that means is that some substantial event from the present will spark a... not madness, but intensity inside of you that will lead to the battle ahead. I can't

explain it to you because you are supposed to experience it for yourself."

Ben fixated on the card resting in the center, "and that one there, what was that again?"

"That is your present, which signified exploring life, love, and all that awaits."

He pulled out his finest attempt at southern charm. "I'd certainly be remiss if I didn't take that as a sign to ask you to dinner."

She paused, contemplating as if someone had just whispered something detrimental in her ear. "I... I don't know if I should." She scrambled across the blanket and reached for a pack of cigarettes.

"You like to smoke, I grow tobacco, see, it's a match made in heaven," Ben said in an attempt to return the joy that had seemingly been sucked from her face.

"I'll think about it." She exhaled a cloud of relief.

He stood. "Well, you said it yourself I am supposed to explore life, love, and ..."

"Okay," she said in a stern voice. "I live a block from here in the only brownstone on Fifth street. Pick me up at eight."

Ben thought back to that day often, wondering if perhaps she had seen a glimmer of her future in his cards, and if she had, why she had agreed to the date.

CHAPTER 7

The Tower

—◦•◦—

Ben stepped off the train and entered the bustling city, aiming for the tall stone building nestled between the park and the river. He could feel the heat of someone's gaze on him as he checked his watch and headed up the stairs.

A voice called from the ground, "Sir, I know you're in a hurry, but could you spare any change?"

He slowed his steps, paused, digging in his coat pocket. "All I have on me," he said while tossing ten dollars into the top hat situated between two men, one with dark hair that fell past his shoulders, the other red-haired and freckles.

The freckled one quickly dug out the bill and heaved the crumpled wad back at him. "Not his fucking money. We don't want his money."

Before the dark-haired one could scramble after it, the first one scolded him like a dog, "Leave it."

"What's wrong with you man?" the long-haired one said with a pouty tone as a nearby stranger plucked the money from the ground.

"Come on, let's get out of here," freckles said before disappearing into the crowd.

Ben paused, questioning the faintly familiar face, shrugged, and continued towards the high rise building where a toothy smile and a handshake awaited in a lobby that boasted architectural statement pieces, a water wall, and a fancy marble desk.

The CEO's right-hand man, otherwise known as slimy Stew, stood properly waiting at reception. His appearance had drastically changed over the years, but that's what happens when people allow themselves to be bought. The once timid intern who came in wearing plastic shoes and a turtleneck had evolved into a powerful assistant, fully equipped with overly tailored designer suits and leather shoes to match. He stopped at nothing to satisfy Sam Stockton, who had groomed him to be his most vigilant employee.

"Ben, Mr. Stockton wanted to meet you here in person, but he was called into a quick meeting," Stew said as they stepped onto the elevator and he scanned the key card that allowed access to the twenty-fourth floor.

"No problem at all."

The over caffeinated man filled the silence between them with his typical pull-string pleasantries... questions that seemed second nature but held no weight at all.

"How was the ride in for you?"

"Just fine, thank you."

He glanced at the numbers, lighting up as they climbed. "I hear you might be working on something new and exciting."

Ben remained silent as the elevator dinged, since he hadn't a clue why he'd been summoned.

"Can I get you something to drink? Coffee?" he asked as they stepped into an executive suite that rivaled any penthouse or boys club.

"I never turn down coffee." He followed Stew to a long marble table surrounded by black leather chairs. Ben looked out the oversized window towards the sparse buildings of the city, none near as nice as the one he stood in, while Stew disappeared for a few moments, quickly returning with a mug of coffee and a binder, placing both upon the table.

"Mr. Stockton will be right in." He smiled before closing the heavy glass door.

Sam appeared more joyful than usual as he entered the room, quickly securing the door behind him. "Like my new suit?" He kicked his red bottomed shoes up on the table while straightening his newest jacket. "I have a meeting this week with some key buyers and want to look sharp."

"Looks expensive."

"It does, doesn't it? Anyway, the reason I called you here is to discuss a new line of cigarettes we're developing along with a new marketing campaign. Remember years ago, when you tried using some sort of ink in the cigarettes? What was it again that appeared on the paper when you lit it?"

"Flowers," Ben huffed. He knew what they were. After all, it was Sam who had soiled the company's reputation and begged Ben to help them creatively bounce back. Ben had spent countless hours trying to get his hands on the patent for a specific heat sensitive ink, only to have the final product squashed by a packaging regulation.

"You've heard of the Plain Packaging Law, haven't you?"

Ben cringed at the reminder of his failure. "You know I have."

"Well, in case you forgot," he said, springing from his chair and walking towards an array of gilt lettered bottles on the bar cart nearby. "Not too long ago, Australia passed a law prohibiting cigarette manufacturers from using specific colors, images, and typefaces on their packaging to make sure they didn't further entice people to buy the product. This got me thinking about the rebranding we've seen in the alcohol industry; same shitty beer, new trendier looking bottle." He poured a few fingers of scotch into a highball glass and continued pacing. "See, if we can latch onto the key triggers of today's youth...well, I think we'll land ourselves in a goldmine."

Ben absorbed that for a moment, took a sip of his coffee, then chuckled.

"Something funny?" Sam's bushy eyebrows drew in.

"The attention span of today's youth is microscopic," Ben said, picturing his son who couldn't hold a conversation for more than two minutes before looking at his phone. "You would need something..."

"Hold that thought." Sam turned as a barrel-chested man entered the room, extending his hand while wearing a devilish grin. "Ben, so nice to meet you."

"And you must be from marketing."

"Pete Tooney," he said as he claimed a seat near the window.

"We were just discussing the attention span of today's youth ..." Sam grinned as though the topic was a pleasant one, when Ben could feel that there was something more sinister in the works.

"Ah yes," Pete said with a grin of his own. "Which is why this concept is so relevant." He slid a flowery gift bag into the center of the boardroom table so that it rested in the space in front of Ben. "In a recent study, a staggering eighty-one percent of consumers sampled something they had never tried before because the packaging caught their eye. Fifty-one percent switched brands entirely because of new packaging." Pete tapped the edge of his binder. "And thank you, by the way, for sending over the information on our additives."

They opened their binders as Pete continued, "What you see in front of you is a summary of our top additives by flavor, and beside it are new findings by demographic." He locked a green-eyed gaze on Ben. "Did you know that forty-three percent of children who had never tried cigarettes before, tried them solely because of the flavors?"

Ben shook his head, trying to keep the disgust from registering on his face. The main thing he hated about his job was that he knew a great deal of his product ended up in the hands of minors, despite the safeguards the government had put in place. "Again, with the children? Haven't we done enough?"

"Sorry, I mean kids ages fifteen to twenty-one." He laughed, but the sound was dismissive and hollow. "The shocking part is when these same kids were asked if they knew if what they were smoking contained nicotine, two-thirds of them said no. So, we're doing something right." Pete smiled widely. "Now, let's turn to the next page."

"What is this?" Ben skimmed over the article, trying to maintain a neutral expression as a tight ball of anxiety lodged in his gut. His family was no different than the ones they deemed as ideal targets. Did they believe that he was so dense that he couldn't see how close to home this hit?

"No need to read the whole thing," Pete said, snatching his attention once again. His tone was so matter of fact that Ben had to grip the edges of the table to stay balanced. "I'll summarize it for you. In a recent study of twenty-five hundred teachers, nearly ninety percent admitted to having a hard time connecting with their students, labelling them as 'an easily distracted generation.' More so, they found that those coming from broken homes were seventy-five percent more likely to experiment with drugs, alcohol, and tobacco."

Ben inhaled and took a long sip of his coffee which was fast cooling beyond an enjoyable temperature. *Distracted generation.* Parents who for one reason or another parted ways, and companies like this one conspiring to capitalize on their children. *Distraction is the least of their problems.*

"The way today's youth processes information is completely different," Pete said. "Think about it ... they are growing up with technology that simply didn't exist when we were kids. So, while others are labelling them as a distracted generation, I am seeing an entirely new group to market to. Turn the page."

Ben struggled to keep a straight face, as he said, "Magic?"

"You won't laugh when you see the numbers."

"And just what role do I play in this... magic pack?" he asked, keeping his voice level.

"Right." Pete reached for the gift bag he had placed upon the table and pulled out a box of perfume. "For weeks now, I've been watching what I believe to be a petty thief practice magic on the streets. Earlier today he 'magically' put a playing card into this unopened box of perfume. I was so mesmerized by the trick, I failed to notice the other items he had stolen from my bag. My fault, I guess." He looked with wishful eyes into the empty bag, half expecting something to reappear. "Which got me thinking about the kids who were unaware that their cigarettes contained nicotine. They were so distracted by the taste and most likely the excitement of trying something new that they completely ignored what was in it." Pete looked towards Ben with wide eager eyes. "My question to you, Ben, is how can we do it? I know you've done something similar before and it didn't quite work out, but what do you say we try it again? Only this time, we'll be smarter about how we present it."

Appalled that his work was being exploited to market cigarettes to struggling teens, he said, "I'm a scientist, not a magician."

Sam lit up with excitement as he poured himself another. "Oh, but you are. You just don't know it yet. If I asked you which one of our additives could turn colors when ignited, what would you say?"

Silence expanded between them so long that he wasn't sure if they'd given him a pass on answering. Their pointed looks at him were so intense that he knew that would never be the case. "We would need to apply a heat sensitive ink," he explained. "Or you could even use an acid-based formula and exhale the smoke onto the cigarette to make the color appear."

Sam and Pete shared a glance, then smiled. Pete spread his hands as he said, "Now imagine this... you light your cigarette and suddenly, there within the paper an image appears; it's the queen of hearts." His eyes grew wide as he warmed up to the idea. One lucky winner will have all of the face cards in their pack. The Queen, King, Jack, and Ace. Think of the social media campaign. Tag us using hashtag magicpack."

"Now, these are just ideas we are talking about. Something like this would require a lot of testing and—"

"You have an entire lab of interns at your disposal," Sam said, clasping a hand on Ben's shoulder. "Let's set up a time to reconvene in two weeks, and you can update us on your progress."

Ben nodded, wanting to shrug the man's hand off his body. "I'll get to work."

* * *

"Do you think he knows?" Sam leaned towards the door, ensuring Ben had disappeared behind elevator doors.

Pete got up from the table and joined him in a celebratory scotch. "He's a simpleton. Simpletons don't think big picture like we do. All he knows is that his once brilliant idea may have a chance to actually work this time. God, can you imagine... dating a woman just to obtain her patents and accidentally getting her pregnant?" Pete said with a villainous laugh.

A staunch grin crept onto Sam's face. "Well, good for him for marrying her."

Pete collected his belongings from the table and headed for the door. "Now all we have to do is make it look like this is

Ben's idea, put him in the limelight, yada yada yada, we sell to children."

Sam slammed down the rest of his scotch and paced the length of the table. "We just can't let him know the real age of kids we're targeting this time. The mention of it nearly gave him a heart attack."

"It's fine." Pete held open the door and flashed a confident smile. "We'll get Ben to create the playing card prototypes we've been after, and then it's off to the races."

Eight of Swords

Brody Tooney was the star quarterback of East Durham High. He never missed a practice, but often missed class. His parent's six figure income had paved the way for him to do just about anything he wanted, all within the well-defined constraints of the town. The things he did, and the things he could be seen doing were two separate things, but today, someone had pushed that boundary.

"Pssst..." a flirtatious whisper called from beneath the bleachers. He squinted through the rungs of metal seats, focusing on the muscular silhouette. Judging by the tan tattooed arms it was Justin, a guy he was sure understood the implications of their actions, yet came anyway. Everything about Justin resembled a young James Dean, handsome, stoic, deliciously rebellious. Annoyance mixed with excitement as he ducked between the seats and joined him.

"What are you doing?" Brody scolded while searching the area for anyone who could spot them. "I told you, never at school."

Justin inched closer, locking his big brown eyes with Brody's. "Sorry, I guess I never was one to follow the rules. I thought I'd catch you before the big game tonight." He leaned in, melting their lips together. Brody placed a hand to his chest pushing him back. "I'm sorry, I can't do this right now. You know I want to but..."

"But you have an image to uphold, I get it." He reached into the worn pockets of his jeans and pulled out a silver cigarette case, finding relief elsewhere. Rumors had already swirled around that the two of them were entirely too close. Neither one of them wanted to add anything more to that mill.

"Allow me." Brody rushed to light Justin's cigarette, taking the first drag. "Chivalry isn't dead to the deserving." Seeing Brody's lips were preoccupied, Justin slid his hand down the front of his pants and whispered, "What else do I deserve?"

Brody's eyes rolled back in his head as Justin loosened his grip. "Oh, come on, I barely touched you."

His laughter ceased as Brody suddenly fell limp, buckling to the ground like a dropped puppet.

"Oh my God, are you okay?"

He shook Brody's shoulder in a frantic panic before scrambling backwards, panting as he scanned the vacant field. The word 'help' screamed through his mind but stopped at his lips. A town this small with minds even smaller would crumble Brody's legacy, and any joy that remained in his parent's lives. He thought back to the countless times he had begged Brody to come out, only to be met with the same two words, 'not yet.'

If he screamed, he would be blasting Brody's secret to the world, and his innocence to the wind. Countless scenarios played out in his mind, all of which ended with him in jail or worse. So, while he wanted so desperately to call for help, he chose not to. Instead, he bolted for the parking lot where the thought of the open road awaited.

With one hand glued to the steering wheel, and the other shaking profusely, he tore through town and sped into the woods, a place they had frequently met. For as fast as he drove, he couldn't escape the thoughts that blew through his mind like the ghost of a blown dandelion.

Did I kill him? No. How could I have?

Attempting to silence his nerves and thoughts he reached into the silver case and retrieved a cigarette. The window refused to roll down any further, the sweat on his face wouldn't dry, and something had to give. He pressed his thumb to the built in lighter, waited for it to glow, then pressed a fresh cigarette to the heat. The sweet taste that haunted his lips stirred up new thoughts, what had killed Brody?

It couldn't have been the cigarettes, otherwise I would be dead too, right?

Justin glanced down at the menacing stick hanging loosely between his fingers.

At least his hands had stopped shaking. He looked up just in time to realize he'd wandered across lanes and was now staring into the bright eyes of an approaching semi.

* * *

Luther ducked beneath the bleachers and made his way towards the body of the young football star. Yellow caution tape encircled the area, barely constraining the droves of people all trying to get a view. Brody's parents rushed across the field with tears streaming down their faces as Luther hurried to instruct the rookie, "Keep them away."

Their sobs faded into the background as Luther knelt by the body, attempting to look away from the blood shot eyes that seemed locked in an eternal scream. There was no blood, no footprints, and no clear sign of a weapon. Nothing to explain why a normal, healthy teenager was now headed to the morgue. He scanned the ground, littered with cigarette butts, his gaze stopping on the one crunched between Brody's fingers. Just as he reached for an evidence bag a beam of light shone through the bleachers. He looked up in annoyance at Sally's eager face peeking through the metal seats.

As soon as she realized his attention was on her, she signaled to the cameraman to begin filming. "This is Sally Childs with Channel Eight News. We're here at East Durham High School where the body of eighteen-year-old football star Brody Tooney has just been located. I'm going to see if we can get any additional information from the Chief of Police who just arrived upon the scene. Sir, can I have a moment?"

Luther glared into the camera as she fired off questions.

"Clearly this death comes as a huge upset to a community already brimming with uncertainty. This is now the sixth death in just a few weeks. Can you tell us, are any of these deaths related? Should we be worried about a potential serial killer?"

He sifted through the land mines she had lobbed at him. "While I cannot provide full answers at this time, I can tell you we are doing all that we can to put the pieces together and figure out just what or who is behind these deaths." He turned, signaling for one of the officers to push her back behind the tape as she threw out one more question.

"I don't see any wounds or evidence of foul play. Can you ascertain the cause of death?"

The wiry-framed coroner hurried onto the scene and slid between the two of them. "Chief, may I have a word in private?"

Sally lingered behind the tape attempting to snag pieces of their conversation. Luther scowled and turned his attention to the coroner who appeared anxious with information.

"I need to talk to you about an oddity I found in the last two autopsies. The lungs of Carl McGinnis and Scott Daniels both held substantial amounts of fluid, which leads me to believe that they ingested something toxic. The other thing that has me troubled are the severe burns in their throats."

Luther answered in a hushed whisper, "Do you think they were poisoned?"

"I do. I also think it was something they inhaled." Their gazes drifted to the same place, locking on the cigarette clenched between Brody's stiff fingers.

Luther was quick to respond, "What about the driver, you know the one with the Porsche? I remember there being an open pack of cigarettes in his car."

The coroner shook his head. "The only toxins found in his body were cocaine and alcohol, but I'm telling you, the last two autopsies..."

"Well, if it is the cigarettes, maybe it's only certain ones?" Luther contemplated in silence. "Nearly every person in this town works for Zamka. Something like this could be detrimental to us." Luther sighed, suspecting this was the work of a criminal mastermind, but he had to wonder if it was one of the anti-tobacco groups or someone with an axe to grind. "I think it best we alert the CDC and ATF."

The coroner exhaled in frustration. "Look, I sent off the specimens for a toxicology report and expect that data to be trusted. When the government comes sniffing, that means money is never far behind. They'll do whatever it takes to protect their friends in big tobacco, and you know it."

Luther lowered his eyes, recalling a similar conversation with the coroner from years prior. He had found traces of poison specific to tobacco plants in the bodies of six children who suddenly went missing and reemerged dead in the river. Once the details surfaced, so did the high paying lawyers, ensuring the voice of justice remained muted. He had himself to blame for the way it was handled, and Sally Childs for the way it was portrayed to the world.

"Don't worry, this will be different."

CHAPTER 9

Queen of Wands

"**H**ey, Andi, can you come here for a second?" Kyle called over his shoulder. "I can't seem to figure out this mixture and could use another set of eyes on it."

"Sure." She lifted the clear goggles and wiped her brow as her lovestruck co-worker focused his eyes on her. "Actually, want to take a quick break? I could use some fresh air."

Kyle swept past the others, grabbed the door and headed out into the hall. She tried to match his long steps which ate up the pavement as he called over his shoulder. "You hear about that football player? Crazy right?"

Kyle's love of everything sports was legendary, including Sports Illustrated Swimsuit edition which he swore was only for reading purposes. "You know I hate sports. Let me guess, everyone is shocked by some horrible thing blah blah blah did? Gooooo Titans!" She hoisted a teetering fist towards the sky, lowering it as they neared the exit.

"I can't believe you didn't hear they found a body under the bleachers at EDH."

That news was swept aside as realization dawned. "I forgot my badge. Do you have yours?"

"Don't need it." He pulled a paperback from his jacket and wedged it between the door. He could always be found reading a murder mystery on lunch and breaks.

She rolled her eyes. "We could get fired. I'll just go back and get it."

"Who's going to tell, the robots? Come on Andi, do you always have to obey the rules?" His taunt was affectionate, but it was enough to halt her steps. She turned back, following the path outside.

Their shoes crunched upon the forest path as they entered the silence of the woods. She wondered who would speak first as they exchanged subtle smiles before returning to their thoughts. The warmth of his breath clashed with the cold sweep that signaled the beginning of another insecure rant.

The last time they were together, Kyle confessed that since the moment he laid eyes on her he had felt inferior. She had transferred from an Ivy League school into the no name town he once felt proud to come from, and slid into an internship that he had fought years to obtain. She had travelled to more places than he knew existed, which he said only added to the richness of her beauty. She was gifted in nearly everything she attempted, from computer code to drawing. On the days when she wasn't studying, she could be found on the hillside near the old, abandoned church overlooking the river. This was her sanctuary, a place where she could sit amongst the overgrowth and let her mind and pencil wander. Within the confines of her sketchpad she had fixed the stained glass of the church, rebuilt the rickety bridge strung over the river, and even sketched a more assertive version of Kyle.

"So, I have to admit I'm a little jealous," Kyle said, breaking the uncomfortable silence.

Andi grinned to hide the awkwardness that welled up within her. "Of what?"

"You."

"Oh yeah? Why's that?" She shoved her hands into her pockets, making sure her fingers didn't fidget and give away her irritation.

"Ben seems to have taken a liking to you." He kicked the gravel in frustration. "Have you noticed that he gives you more attention than the rest of us?"

Those words held some truth. Ben had been inviting her to complete random tasks, assist with the cameras, and even partake in new studies unbeknownst to the others, but rightfully so. Andi was too smart to be in this program, even smarter than Ben in some areas. The truth of it was, she was only here for one reason... to perfect the science of addiction and find even better ways to combat it. What better way to defeat an enemy than learning the methods said enemy employed? While she'd never divulge the truth of her intentions to Ben, she knew she was appreciated for the wealth of fresh knowledge she brought to the lab.

"I think you're confusing attention with requests for help." She smirked but didn't quite meet his accusatory gaze.

"Then why do you leave with him all of the time?" His tone had thickened and suddenly his questioning didn't seem so innocent any longer.

Andi turned to face him, frightened by the thought that Kyle might believe Ben was sleeping with her. Those kinds of whispered rumors could derail a woman's career. Every advance would seem suspect. "If I tell you something, you can't tell anyone else okay?"

He nodded.

"We're developing a new line of cigarettes and Ben asked me to help create the prototypes. I come in early once a week to work in his private lab."

Kyle's head titled as he peered down at her. "Private lab?"

"I promised him I wouldn't tell anyone about it," she whispered, wondering if she had chosen the wrong time to trust Kyle with something so important. Normally she didn't keep things from him. This shouldn't be any different, but ... "So, you have to keep this a secret okay?"

"Well..."

"Well what?" she demanded.

"Nothing." He shrugged, gesturing toward the building. "We'd better get back. I think Ben said he wanted to talk to us before he leaves."

They returned as silently as they had left, sliding in, removing the book, and allowing the door to close completely.

"You really need to stop doing that," she scolded.

He placed a hand to his heart in dramatic fashion. "Forgive me?"

"Only if you cook dinner for me." His pause gave her the ability to walk ahead of him, and hope that throwing that at him would buy his complete confidence.

"Wait, what? I get another date?" He hurried behind, halting any further conversation as they entered the lab.

Several pairs of eyes turned, noticing the awkwardness of their arrival as Ben stood silently waiting, his lips set in a thin line of disapproval. His keen gaze swept over them as though trying to find the wrong reason for them to be coming back so late.

"Now that everyone is here, we can begin," he said, and his tone signaled his impatience. "I recently had a meeting at corporate. As of this moment, we will be focusing our energy on a new product being prototyped. Using cutting edge technology and a new heat sensitive ink, you will be creating cigarettes with images that appear on the paper once ignited." He walked around the room placing a binder at each student's station. "Within this packet you will find all that you need to know about the design you are to create. Each of you has been assigned a specific image that needs to appear on the cigarette when lit. Do you understand?"

Eyebrows raised in silent judgement as they thumbed through their packets.

A hand shot up and Ben nodded toward Kyle, who asked, "Why playing cards?"

Ben shrugged. "These designs were chosen by corporate, and from what I understand one of you *may* be chosen to present your design to the CEO of Zamka Tobacco, Sam Stockton." He headed for the door. "Oh, and when you're done, place your finished product into an envelope, sign it, and leave it at your station."

"Looks like you're not so special after all," Kyle whispered, and there was a tone of triumph in his words.

Andi sulked to her station, disheartened by the level of Kyle's immaturity. She skimmed through the contents of her binder. "Mr. Flowers, I have a quick question."

When he moved past Kyle and the others, she lowered her voice to a mere whisper. "This looks different than what I've been working on for you."

"Is that a question?" he asked, his steely gaze narrowing on her.

"I mean, do you still need my help?" she asked, adjusting her stance under the heat of Kyle's watchful eyes.

Ben paused for a long few moments before giving her a fatherly pat on the back. "Until I say otherwise. Oh, and between you and me," he said, leaning in so only she would hear. "I'll be presenting your queen of hearts design to corporate. So, when you're done, just leave it on your desk and I'll personally come and pick it up."

Andi watched his progression until he disappeared into the hallway. Kyle's focus was on her and his scowl signaled he was not elated at the exchange.

Ten of Swords

"**H**ey Ben." Linda nosed her way into the breakroom. "Supposed to snow today, you want a ride home?"

He checked his watch, realizing he'd been tucked away in the private lab so long that time had flown by. "Is it that time already? I'm fine on my bike, but I'd better get going. Tristan and his girlfriend are coming for brunch today." He gathered his things and hurried down the hall.

"Wow, all these years and he's never brought a girl home. She must be special." Linda followed behind, fumbling through her purse for the keys to her Trans Am.

He paid no mind to the ill-timed flurries falling from the sky as he hopped on his bike and disappeared down the old country road. Early snow meant damaged crops and lost revenue. Something unheard of in the South until about a decade ago. *There's no such thing as curses* he reminded himself, as he passed the fork in the road and headed into the acres of tobacco that surrounded his home.

As he sped through the miles of dying crops, Iris came to mind. The love of his life. The woman that Maggie could never replace. The woman who had no clue she was still wreaking havoc in his life.

His life had fallen apart the moment Iris' mind unraveled and they hauled her off to the psych ward, leaving his oldest son bearing a grudge that still haunted him to this day . . .

"Ben, please don't do this to me."

His heart broke with every word.

Black makeup smeared down her face as she cried. "Just because you don't understand something doesn't make it wrong."

"You're talking to people who simply aren't there, and now you've set fire to the farm." He could still hear the sounds of the crackling fire as it engulfed miles of tobacco plants ready for harvest. He cringed as her words burned in his memory.

"What you and your company have done to those children is unforgivable." She accused in a glare that made him shudder. "This is your fault Ben."

Everything Ben had done since his first marriage had imploded was to make up for the wrong he'd created by allowing Sam to source the labor for the farm. No one knew how evil their plans had been. And thanks to the fact the company had some high-powered lawyers and never-ending bank accounts, they had gotten away with everything.

Ben planned to change all of that.

He was nearly home when the faint outline of a man, madly flailing his arms, came into focus. All thoughts of his former family swept from his mind as reality stretched out before him.

"Oh no." He kicked the cycle in gear and sped towards the familiar car pulled halfway off the road at an unnatural angle.

"Dad," Tristan screamed. The sound was so filled with angst that it made the hairs on Ben's neck stand up.

"What's the matter?" He parked his bike beside the running car.

"It's ... it's ... Summer, she... she's not breathing." Tears soaked his face as he yanked open the car door, her lifeless body falling limp into his arms. "I called for help already."

"Tell me exactly what happened." Ben angled toward the body, trying to remain composed enough for the both of them.

"I ... I don't know" Tristan stammered while staring into Summer's cold vacant eyes attempting to formulate thoughts.

"This is important son, think now." He flashed a glance towards the tattoos peeking out from under her leather jacket. "I don't mean to intrude here, but did she smoke anything?"

"What?" Tristan's head whipped towards Ben, eyes wide with shock. "You think we were doing drugs?"

"It's just that I smell smoke." Ben reached a steady hand into the car, pulling out what remained of a cigarette that was burning a hole in the seat cushion.

"She was nervous to meet you guys." He knelt beside her and took hold of her hands. "Today was supposed to be so special," he sobbed.

The sound of sirens carried from the distance as Tristan's snowy tracks traced around the car. Ben placed a calming hand on his shoulder, halting his movements. "It's freezing out here, why don't you go on in the house."

Tristan flickered a gaze to Summer, then trudged to the driver's side and returned to his rightful place beside her. He doubled over with his head in trembling hands, confessing plans for marriage, and other broken endeavors. Flashes of red and blue blurred through the snow as a man approached the car, tapping on the window.

The Chief of Police peered in. "Tristan?"

"Hey Luther," he greeted, wiping the tears away with the back of his hand.

"You mind stepping out of the car and telling me what happened? Uh, how about over here?" He walked towards the field as the emergency crew attempted to work on Summer's body.

Luther whipped out a notepad from the inside pocket of his jacket and patiently waited for Tristan's attention.

"We were on our way to my dad's for breakfast. I picked Summer up at her apartment, and then we stopped at the market to pick up a few things." He looked over Luther's shoulder towards the car, hope dimming from his eyes with every passing second. "We were almost here when all of the sudden it was as if she couldn't breathe. She was just gasping for air. I slammed on the brakes and the car slid sideways. Then, everything just … stopped."

Luther looked up from his notepad. "Did she have any medical conditions? Asthma?"

"Not that I know of."

"Do you know what she did earlier today?"

Tristan rubbed his temples trying to think of anything other than the present. "We woke up, left my apartment, grabbed some coffee near her house. She walked home from there and my friend Kyle came to meet me for a bit of studying until it was time for me to pick her up."

Luther scribbled a few more notes. "Is there anything else you'd like us to know about Summer? Anything at all, Tristan?"

"I was going to ask her to marry me..." He lowered his head as the loss hit him all over again.

Luther stepped away and pulled Ben into a hushed whisper, "The coroner's going to be here in a few. I'm going to need you to take the boy inside while they do their work. Don't come back out until we're gone, understand? Seeing the body taken away is always hard. I just don't want that to be a memory Tristan holds onto."

Ben attempted to corral Tristan towards the driveway, but he broke free from his grasp, making a break for the car. Luther lunged, throwing his arms around Tristan's back while talking him down. "You need to go inside son. I know this is hard, but that's what I need you to do."

With tears nearly frozen to his face, Tristan retreated towards home as Luther turned to Ben. "I'll be in touch tomorrow, probably have him come down to the station to give a formal statement. If you have any questions, call my cell."

"Thanks, buddy." Ben patted him on the back before retrieving his son. Together they disappeared up the drive as Maggie ran from the house, her steps big and awkward as she navigated the freezing snow.

"What happened?" she screeched, gripping the edges of Ben's jacket. "I was setting the table when I saw the lights outside. Is anyone hurt?" She craned her neck to look past him towards the frantic activity then returned to Tristan's tear-soaked face.

"Where's Summer?" Her focus trailed between the ambulance and the car. "Oh no, oh what happened?" She released Ben and threw her arms around Tristan. "Come on, get inside."

The minute the three of them made it across the threshold, Tristan said, "I need to be alone." His steps were slow and measured as he sulked upstairs towards his old bedroom.

They waited for the creaks in the floorboards to subside before moving toward the dining room and Maggie asked, "What happened out there, Ben?"

Ben relayed what he learned from Tristan as she placed a hand over her heart. "That's horrible. Any clue as to what caused it? Was she sick?"

He shook his head, but all sorts of scenarios were running through his mind. The mysterious fires, the football player, the motel death. Now Summer. He couldn't fathom that his special package had somehow ... no, he wouldn't think that. His plan had been foolproof.

"Seems she was healthy," Ben said, while searching the cabinets for something sweet. "But who knows. I'm sure Luther will get to the bottom of it. Worst part of it all .... he was going to ask for her hand."

"Poor Tristan." She wiped the tears from her eyes using one of the cloth napkins she insisted on having at every meal. "I bet you're starving. Here, let me make you a plate."

They sat at the table in silence, barely touching the meal as the flashing lights finally faded from the street. She looked over Ben's shoulder towards the muted television, where another tragedy was being told. "Just can't get away from it."

He turned to take in the elements of the newscast, broadcasting, "Forty car pileup, seventeen dead," when the phone rang.

"I'll get it," he hurried down the hall towards his office, putting distance between his wife's grief, the tragedy playing out on the highway, and the sinking feeling that something had gone horribly wrong.

"Hello?"

"Ben, it's Sam. Sorry to call you at home, but I need you to come into town tomorrow morning for an emergency meeting at eight."

"But... I'll just be getting off work then."

"Alright," he quipped. "Then make it half past."

Ben looked out the window towards the accumulating snow. "Could you send a car?"

He hung up the phone, and waited a moment to see if Maggie had somehow inched down the hall in her typical fashion to listen in. Hearing no sign of her, he reached into the bookshelf and retrieved a hidden cell phone. He dialed. The continued ringing heightened his nerves as he scowled and confessed his frustration to voicemail.

"Hey. This is... you know who this is. Listen, I need to make sure that those packages were delivered as instructed. Call me back."

CHAPTER 11

The Hanged Man

—◆◆◆—

"**S**o glad you could make it on such short notice." Sam hurried to close the heavy oak door to his office before pouring a glass of scotch from his not so secret cabinet. Ben took his seat in the chair across from his desk, thankful for the coffee that awaited him. He'd had a restless night and it certainly showed on his face. All of the deaths and the areas where they played out could not be a coincidence. This was not how things were supposed to happen.

"Open the binder."

He downed a shot as Ben combed through the graphic images.

"What... what is this?" He averted his gaze.

"These people all died suddenly within the last few weeks, and they all have one thing in common. The last thing they did was smoke a cigarette." He poured himself another drink.

Chills crawled up Ben's spine while he tried to steady his breathing. "I don't think I follow."

"I received a phone call from the ATF. This could be coincidence, but I think something serious is going on and I want our brand as far away from these headlines as possible."

Ben glanced at the binder one last time. "Whatever I can do to help, just say the word."

"I'll need you to conduct an in-depth analysis of our product; pull the reports from the machines and check the additives, ratios, packaging quality, and dates of shipment. The more information the better. I already have someone working to get us the toxicology reports from the coroner's office." Sam wiped the beads of sweat forming on his face with his silk pocket square. "I honestly don't know what to make of it. You've worked here for thirty years. You know better than anyone that we make quality products. We certainly aren't responsible for killing people."

Ben concealed his derision, yearning to point out the obvious. They *had* killed people. Children, to be exact. They should have never been in the fields in the first place, but then again Sam always had a way of going behind Ben's back to find cheap labor. The greed that poured from this business was enough to fill a river, which ironically was where those children ended up.

"There's a warning on the label stating that it may do just that..."

"Suppose there is," Sam countered, setting the glass next to the coaster instead of on it.

"Don't worry, Sam." Ben closed the binder. "I'll get the data to you as soon as possible, and I'll need to see whatever test results come from the victims. In the meantime, if there is anything I can do, please let me know."

"Do not tell a soul about this," he warned. "And when you've finished collecting the data put it on a drive and bring it directly to me."

* * *

"I'll just be a moment," Ben instructed the driver as they neared the plant. He cringed at the thought of being there during the day shift, but the thought of waiting another day to pull the reports weighed heavy on his mind.

The floor was oddly busy with unusual guests, examining machines, taking notes, interviewing employees. Ben's gaze remained lowered as he headed for the IT closet and quickly locked the door behind him. The chill of the server room was a refreshing reminder of the looming fear that had him so rattled. He wiped his forehead and inserted the thumb drive. As the downloads scanned across the screen, the images from the binder flashed in his mind.

That many cigarette deaths within the same town all within three weeks' time ... could something have happened with the packages?

A loud beep interrupted his downward spiral of thoughts as the word, 'complete' flashed upon the screen. He grabbed the drive and headed back towards the parking lot, questioning if he should have a look around.

He walked through the warehouse towards his private lab, where Andi was in the process of examining something underneath a microscope. He scanned the top corners of the room, noticing something was a little off as he quietly closed the door behind him ensuring she remained consumed in her work. As he leaned over her shoulder, his shadow must have given him away.

"Oh my God." She yanked her headphones from her ears, nearly falling off the stool. "How long have you been there?" she said with a nervous laugh.

"Not long." He eyed the loose tobacco underneath the microscope and the bottles of ink beside it. "What are you working on?"

"I ... um, there was something unusual in the lab and Kyle asked me to take a look at it for him."

Ben thought that over for a minute, pulled up a stool beside her, and examined the dissected cigarette for himself. "Did he now? Tell me about this oddity, I love a good puzzle."

Her jaw dropped and she seemed to shrink under his glare. "I... I didn't find anything."

"Funny how people can stir our minds into a frenzy," he said, giving her a reassuring smile.

"It's just that there are cops here questioning people and examining our products, and Kyle read an article in the paper about some sort of disease killing people..." She lowered her head. "I'm sorry, I just wanted to see for myself."

Since the moment that Ben had agreed to help Tristan's friend obtain an internship that he was hardly qualified for, he had regretted it. Kyle McGinnis was a constant distraction to Andi, and always trailed behind on assignments. Now, he had meddled in a very private project that no one else was supposed to know about. These were things he had entrusted her with, things that not even she was to fully understand. With the recent tragedy that had claimed the lives of Kyle's family, his grief had evolved into frequent outbursts, hostile meltdowns, and now this.

Ben retrieved the binder he had given her and collected what remained of the coded cigarettes. He scanned the room for other out of place items, and stopped upon the open cages.

Before he could ask the whereabouts of the mice she stammered, "They were healthy this morning and when I came back from lunch, they were dead. I buried them out back."

"Have you ever heard of The Black Death?"

Andi's eyes went blank. Still, he waited a few seconds before proceeding. "More commonly known as the Black Plague, a rapidly spreading disease that wiped out tens of millions of people between 1347 and 1351." He walked the room, slowly picking up test tubes and setting them back on the shelves. "People would wake up healthy in the morning and be dead by evening. It was responsible for removing nearly half of Europe's population. While the plague was a horrible disease, what emerged from its chaos was a much healthier society."

"What do you mean?" she asked, fidgeting with her headphones.

Ben reclaimed the seat he had vacated. "Fewer people meant less demand for food and housing, and as a result the prices of goods dropped. Wages increased by three times after the plague, which allowed people to buy and sell higher quality foods. People ate better, lived healthier lives, and had more money to provide for their families."

"Why are you telling me this?" she asked, turning to face him.

"Would you look at the time," he said, faking a yawn. "It's been quite a long day, and I have a car waiting."

Her gaze remained on the specimen as he called over his shoulder, "Oh, and Andi, would you turn the cameras back on? Someone must have *accidentally* turned them off."

He walked out the door and didn't wait around to hear her excuses.

CHAPTER 12

The Devil

—●··●··●—

"What was that noise?"

Maggie shot up in bed and wrapped her night coat around her shoulders. "You heard it didn't you?" She reached for the lamp on the nightstand as Ben grabbed her hand, stilling her movements.

"Stay here and keep the lights off." He pulled his pistol and a flashlight from beneath his side of the bed.

"Be careful," she whispered as he disappeared down the hall, moving towards Tristan's room.

"Good, I didn't wake you. I think I heard something outside. Stay here with your mother."

His feet creaked upon the old floorboards as he searched the house, checking each room before heading for the front door. Silent as a shadow, he slipped outside, walking the perimeter. He directed his flashlight upon the fresh tire tracks where a poorly wrapped package lay in the mud.

"Aren't you clever," he said, examining the hand rolled cigarette with what looked like coordinates and a time, faintly written upon the paper.

"Ben?" Maggie called from the porch. "Everything okay?"

He tucked it into his palm. "Well, if it wasn't you'd be in trouble for paying no mind to my instructions."

"I couldn't help myself," she whined.

"It's alright." He crossed the driveway and wrapped his arms around his shivering wife. "Come on now, let's get back inside."

She peered over his shoulder. "Are those tire tracks? Was someone here?"

He nodded. "Don't worry; I'll take care of it."

"Are you sure everything is okay?"

"It's fine I said. Now get back to bed before you catch a cold."

She walked halfway up the stairs before calling down to him, "It's Sunday, you can go back to bed, you know?"

"I'm going to stay up... need to go take care of something."

* * *

"Interesting choice for a meeting place." Ben stepped from his bike and walked towards the scrawny silhouette leaned against the only light post at the gas station.

Kyle puffed out his chest. "I'd say the same to you. After all, the coordinates written on the cigarette were copied from one you just had Andi make in your *private little lab*."

Ben was glad that the shadows covered his expression as his anger at Andi's inability to keep a secret threatened to surface.

"I checked all of the ones written in that binder you gave her," Kyle said, his blue eyes intense with accusations. "And each one corresponds to a train station, airport, or seedy gas station like this one." He gestured to the rickety place behind them. "So, tell me Ben, what's so special about these places?"

Ignoring the implications behind questions, he casually asked, "Why are you in my program, Kyle?"

"Because, just like you, I am fascinated with addiction."

Ben laughed. "You think that's why I work for Zamka? I'm not fascinated with addiction, I detest it."

Kyle's angular face took on a distorted expression. "Well, then you sure picked an interesting place to work."

Ben narrowed his eyes on the pompous twerp. "Okay Kyle, here's one for you. A woman repeatedly went to the hospital, always demonstrating the same symptoms—dizziness, fatigue, vomiting, and cognitive impairment. It wasn't until her seventh visit that they realized her COhb levels had spiked at around twenty-seven percent. Eventually, her habits led to long-term cognitive impairment, and a coma. Addiction consumed her, reduced her to almost nothing."

Kyle shrugged as though none of this held any consequence. "So, she was an addict, lots of people are."

"But does it make her less of a person?"

Kyle looked smug at the thought. "Of course it doesn't. She's a human and humans make mistakes."

"What I'm asking is, how many times can you make the same mistake before realizing the consequences?"

Kyle smiled, and a flash of triumph lit in his eyes. "Do the consequences include being institutionalized?"

Ben's eyes narrowed in on him upon hearing those words. If he could put his hands around Kyle's neck and squeeze the life out of him it wouldn't be soon enough. How dare he bring up something so sensitive and private.

"Funny what things you can find when you really start digging." Kyle smirked, and his gaze never strayed from Ben's face.

"You know what they say about digging, eventually you find yourself at the bottom of a hole. Step foot on my property again and it will be your last time," he warned as he walked back towards his motorcycle.

"You may have blinders on Andi, but I'm on to you and whoever else is in on this game you're playing." He tried to catch up to Ben. "I won't stop until I figure it out."

"Goodbye Kyle."

Ben maneuvered the bike around him and took off for home, realizing he had more problems than he originally thought.

* * *

Ben mulled over this new wrinkle in his plans as he retreated into the welcomed comfort of the countryside. If Kyle had been more emotionally stable, or even half as smart as Andi, he could work him into the equation somehow, but it just didn't seem possible. He was getting too close to information that should have never made it into his hands. He mentally shifted the blame to Andi... whatever happened next would be her fault.

A flashing light came from behind, interrupting his thoughts. He checked his rearview, catching a glimpse of Luther's face as he pulled over.

"Ben."

"Luther."

"Sorry to stop ya," he said, his typically clean-cut face covered in stubble. "How's your boy doin'?"

Ben repositioned on the seat. "As expected, but he's young."

"Ben I gotta ask you something and I need you to be straight with me. In all the years you've worked at Zamka, have you ever once thought that someone might tamper with your products?"

"No sir, but it seems like the ATF may think otherwise. I'm worried about my family... my job..."

Luther sighed before sharing what should have been private information. "We've called in the CDC for an investigation of the toxins we've found in the last four bodies. There's a lot of theories floating around, but they seem to think something got to the water supply... maybe from the plastic company."

"Water supply?"

Luther shrugged. "That's what they think. I've looked after this town nearly all my life, and I refuse to let my people down. I'm gonna find out what is causing this if it kills me."

"You don't owe East Durham anything, Luther. I know you feel responsible for the way that court case played out, but you can't keep holding your feet to the fire. It's time to forgive yourself and let it go."

Luther shook his head, then headed back towards his cruiser while calling over his shoulder. "Give Maggie my regards and tell her I'll be keeping an eye on you guys. You're like family to me."

"Thanks." Ben called to the reflection in the mirror. "But you know we can handle our own."

He paused before getting into the car. "I know. Just thought you should know I'm watching."

Luther's cruiser faded into the distance as Ben sped towards home where Maggie stood waiting by the door.

"Ben." She flung her arms around him. "You were gone all night."

"What's gotten into you?" He looked past her into the living room where the sound of the television blared.

"I'm so glad you're okay," she said against the wall of his chest.

"In here," Tristan called from the den where he stood with feet glued to the floor and remote clenched in hand.

"There's a disease. It's everywhere. Good, healthy everyday people ... teachers, store clerks, doctors—they're all dropping dead."

'*Teacher found dead at local school,*' displayed across the bottom of the screen as Sally Childs interviewed the teacher's sobbing coworker.

"I know this is hard for you, but can you tell us what happened here today?" Sally said.

The coworker took a deep breath before answering, "We... we had just finished eating lunch, and went out for a short walk before our next class, and then all of the sudden she just collapsed. It happened so quick." Tears returned to her eyes as they panned back to Sally.

"As you can see, it's been a hard day for many people who are all desperately searching for answers. Back to you."

Tristan scanned the channels, each story more tragic than the last. Maggie's eyes glazed over with tears as she watched a little boy holding a dirty teddy bear cling to his mother's leg. "We were walking to the store when a car came up on the curb and... my husband." She sobbed into her hands as the camera focused on the flashing ambulance lights behind them.

The reporter ran towards the EMT as they shut the doors. "Sir, can you tell us anything about what happened here today? Is everyone okay?" she blurted, trying to catch up to the hurried strides of the man whose scowl showed his frustration at being questioned when he had much more important things to address.

"Ma'am, we don't have time to do this right now. All I can tell you is the taxi driver is deceased, and the man he struck needs to get to the hospital. Now, please move."

Ben walked to the television and powered it down. "Doesn't do us any good watching this."

"Well, what else are we supposed to do?" Tristan threw the remote onto the couch and stormed upstairs.

Maggie attempted to bring joy to at least one person in the house and threw on an apron. "You must be starving, let me make you something to eat."

Ben watched her move around the kitchen, cleaning behind her every move. Though, this time her compulsion seemed a touch more excessive than normal. She made an entire meal in record time and the kitchen showed no sign of it.

"Everything okay, Maggie?"

She set a plate of sausage, eggs, grits, biscuits, and a cup of coffee in front of him. "Mmmm hmmm."

"You sure?"

Ben settled in his chair and watched her, wondering what was going on in that anxious mind of hers.

She exhaled. "Look, I think something's wrong with the accounts. I balanced the checkbook three times and somehow there's more money... like, a *lot* more money. I know it's not a bad problem to have, but it's just odd."

Ben flashed to any number of explanations but settled on something closer to the truth. "Forgot to tell you, I cashed in an old bond." He paused to sip his coffee. "Was going to surprise you with a vacation." He gave her what he hoped was a reassuring smile. "But I guess the cat is out of the bag."

"There's something else..." She tossed a crumpled note on the table. "Who is Jake?"

CHAPTER 13

The Sun

Sally Childs waited patiently outside of the coroner's office for the man she was certain held answers. Despite the freezing rain, she stood with cell phone in hand, eager to record a conversation that could change the trajectory of her career. She had been on a downward spiral of dead-end stories and her lackluster reputation only made it worse. It used to be that her only goal was to be in the limelight and develop a resume that would land her a job on a major network. Fate seemed to have a different plan, and continued to put her in the same place at the same time as then officer Luther Cooper; their frequent interactions turned into frequent dinners, and then more. She cringed recalling how their relationship ended, with a screaming match that took place right where she now stood. He had trusted her with information on those kids, and shared things in the privacy of the bedroom that never should have made it onto television. That's the thing about trusting people who love their careers more than others: you can't.

Frank Timmons was a wiry man in a wrinkly oversized suit, with a strange haircut and distant eyes that had seen some things. He shuffled past her, eager to get to his next destination, which tonight was the Irish pub at the end of the block.

"Hello? Frank?" Sally hurried down the sidewalk after the man that was quick to dismiss her. "It's me, Sally, I'm from Channel 8 News. I just wanted to ask you a few questions if that's okay?"

He smugly called over his shoulder, "if you want to talk to me, I'll be in here."

Aside from the regular patrons whose names appeared on the silver plaques where they were usually positioned night after night, the typically packed college bar was quiet.

Everything about this place offended Sally's senses. The smell of stale beer made her nose twitch; equally as obnoxious were the flashing neon signs and blaring Irish folk music. The bartender busied himself with cleaning, though it was apparent the mirrors, shelves, and bottles hadn't seen a good wipe down in ages. Sally brushed what appeared to be crushed peanuts from the barstool beside Frank and took her seat. Before she could ease into pleasantries, he swirled his finger towards the barkeep, signaling his usual order of a light beer.

"Keep em' coming," he said, knocking back the first one in a matter of seconds. His down-in-one-sip demeanor certainly added to her existing line of questions. The roar of the television chased his attention and he scanned the multiple screens for something of interest, as Sally pulled her cell phone from her purse.

"So, Frank, and by the way this is off the record. I see you're pretty upset about something. I don't want to annoy you any further but..."

He slammed down another beer and wiped his mouth with the paper napkin that held the bar's logo. "You're here just in time actually. Not like I have to worry about much. Retirement's right around the corner." He sighed, settling his gaze on the football game. "You know what the problem with this town is? It's a good old boys town, and good old boys always cover things up for one another." He raised the glass toward the television displaying another report on the mysterious deaths. "I've been saying for weeks that the deaths are related to cigarettes, and now they've called in the CDC and ATF who seem to think something got dumped into the water. There's nothing wrong with the water." He laughed before downing another. "Not like I drink it anyhow. Give me some good old eighty proof any day."

"So, you're saying that there could be a problem with the water supply?"

Frank looked at her with unamused eyes. "No. I'm saying that if there were something in the water I'd still be at work. The last six autopsies I've done all showed signs of pulmonary edema with severe burning in the mouth and throat. I can scream to the heavens that the cause of death is respiratory failure and still they will go on to investigate the water. Like I said, good old boys club."

"Would you be willing to go on camera and share this information?" She picked up her cell phone, ready to record.

"Hold that thought." He slammed back another and smacked his lips thoughtfully. "You betcha."

She paused, lowering the phone for a second. "You know what you are about to say is going to affect every person that lives in this town in one way or another right?"

Frank held up the glass, put it back down on the counter and nodded. "The people need to know the truth. If my memory serves me right, you're just the lady to give it to them."

Sally tried to tamp down on her elation as she said, "And... go."

CHAPTER 14

King of Swords

———◆··◆··◆———

Ben hurried into the near empty subway while mentally dissecting the recent events that had spiraled out of control. A long list of very specific people should have received those packages. Clearly none of them had, since they were all still drawing an untimely breath. Things would hit differently if their families were the ones being impacted.

Now with the ATF breathing down his back and everyone at Zamka Tobacco, he had to ensure all loose ends were tied and nothing would lead back to him. Unfortunately, he had to tread even more carefully than before. Couldn't blame the machines for this one.

He moved towards the silhouette of a man seated on the ground with his back against the wall. An oversized black hoodie concealed his face, which was sure to match the dirty hands that shuffled an odd deck of cards.

A few scattered people hurried past. The echoes of their footsteps seemed a bit more intense given the emptiness of the tunnels. *Where was everyone?*

The fluorescent lights flickered as Ben neared, causing an eerie laugh to escape the man's lips.

"Something funny?" Ben called out, tracing his hands over the place where his favorite pocket watch used to hang.

"Time..." The stranger kept his head lowered and continued shuffling.

"I'm sorry?" Ben grew angered by his elusiveness.

"Is this your card?" He flipped up a familiar card depicting a goddess with arms raised above her head.

"Where'd you get that?" Ben said, narrowing his gaze on the man.

Jake looked up from under his hood, his pointed glare like a dagger to Ben's heart.

"It was a gift," he answered, and the contempt in his voice wasn't hard to miss. "One that showed me your sad, lonely, and jobless future."

"Ahh, now I recognize you." He scowled. "I believe you've mistaken my life for your own." Ben attempted to tamp down on the disgust rearing up at the state his son had settled in. A drastic decision made shortly after Ben told him his mother had passed away. Now he was on the street instead of in school or working, and seemed to be all alone.

"You know, they say that when significant trauma occurs in someone's life," Jake began, "It's as if a record that continuously plays the same melody suddenly skips, forcing the brain into a new channel." Jake reached for the old pocket watch sitting beside the cards, the one precious item he couldn't bring himself to sell. "So...thank you for the trauma you've caused me father. You've opened my eyes to things I never knew existed." He laughed, but there was no humor in the sound. "No wonder mom could never sleep. Especially with all the souls your company exchanged for that almighty dollar dancing around her head like paper dolls."

Ben flashed back to the image of the burning field as Iris' words echoed in his mind, *"this is your fault Ben." Days before she had set the crops ablaze, she had gone for a walk through the field. She said there were voices that called her out there, and perhaps they had.*

"Don't make light of her illness; may she rest in peace," Ben growled as his skin flushed with heat.

"You're still calling it an illness?" Jake shook his head. "I have visions too you know, and if you'd open your eyes you'd see it's a gift not a curse."

"Probably from all the crap that you put in your body. You know, if you'd just stayed home..."

Resentment wrinkled through his brow. "I would have been a part of your despicable lies, and trust me when I say, my visions have shown me all of them." He rose, looking Ben square in the eyes. "What's that type of death called again, when your body absorbs the toxins from tobacco plants?" Ben remained silent, responding with only a scowl. "Green... green something." He shrugged. "I guess what matters is that you hauled the person that found the bodies off to the psych ward, but she did try to talk... didn't she?"

"That's enough." Ben flashed back to the moment a surprise witness was brought into the courtroom.

Dark roots had crept over her bleach blonde hair, slowly stripping away what elements remained of her personality. Her face appeared pale and weathered by tears, and her cool blue eyes glassy as a lake in winter. The courtroom grew silent as she slinked onto the stand and locked her eyes on the man responsible.

Her icy glare remained fixated on Ben as Zamka's high priced attorneys fired off question after demeaning question.

"Mrs. Flowers, is it true that you heard voices calling from the field, and when you walked out into the tobacco field you found the bodies of all six children?" There was a smugness to his tone as he turned and looked to the jury with wide eyes.

He was rewarded by a few giggles, as the judge smacked her mallet.

"Order. Go ahead Mrs. Flowers."

She looked towards her doctor for approval. "I was told I can testify on some matters, just not my own...condition." The doctor nodded as she continued. "So, I can't tell you why I walked out into the field, only that I did, and that's where I found them."

Her words triggered sobs from the grieving parents as Ben lowered his head in shame. She looked to Luther, searching for a mirror of the truth. "That's when I ran inside and called the police."

The attorney paced before the lectern. "You say you called the police, but we show no record of you calling 911."

She quipped, "That's because I didn't call 911, I called Officer Cooper."

"And why did you do that?" All eyes shifted to Luther.

"Because he's been a friend of the family for years and I trusted him."

The attorney scoffed. "And yet, he too has no recollection of the call or finding these bodies in your field. We heard from Officer Cooper just moments ago that he found the bodies in the river."

She shook her head. "That's not where he found them."

"Did the voices tell you that?" he slipped out tauntingly as the judge intervened. "Order."

Jake interrupted his trip down memory lane. "I see them too you know... those children you put out in the fields." He looked over Ben's shoulder to the empty platform. Vibrations echoed around them. "Do you want to know what they're saying right now?"

"That you're insane?" Ben turned his head towards the approaching train as Jake pressed the pocket watch to his ear.

"They're saying that your time's almost up, and one day you're going to wish you knew a trick, any trick, to make it all stop."

Despite Jake's wild claims he was oddly right. Everything Ben had done since that tragic day had resulted in chaos and failure. Some part of him wondered if this was the battle Iris had seen in the cards so many years ago.

Ben rushed forward and stepped onto the train as the doors closed, calling to his son as he fled. "Hey Jake, you know the best thing about magic?"

Jake's expression went blank.

"If you're good at it, no one ever finds out how you did it."

* * *

"Hey, man. What are you doing?" Ricky ran down the stairs as Jake collected his cards from the ground.

"I don't know," he said, burying his emotions about his father. "Hoping to make a few bucks, but it's a ghost town."

"Because you're in the wrong place. Come on, opportunity is literally waiting for you up there. Hurry, this way." Ricky's pace quickened as they entered the streets, ducking into_an alleyway towards the roar of the crowd filled with picket signs and protesters screaming their claims to the opposing side.

Anti-tobacco enthusiasts surrounded Zamka's corporate office while chanting "shut down poison town" all while hundreds of former Zamka employees replied, "No cigarettes! No work!"

Both sides were equally ripe for the picking. Jake and Ricky mixed into the crowd stealing a credit card here, a wallet there, and if they were lucky maybe even a set of car keys. They hadn't seen this much easy cash since Oktoberfest. While this event didn't provide free beer or pretzels, it was just as enjoyable and even more profitable. Among it all was Sally Childs, attempting to capture both sides of the quickly unfolding story.

Chants surged through the air as a hefty man, too young to be missing teeth, pushed his way onto camera. "I'm sick and tired of all this fake news, there ain't nothing wrong with the cigarettes. And now, we're out of work." He slicked the sparse whiskers from his lips while trying to catch a breath. "What, a handful of people die and all of the sudden they shut down the economy? This whole thing is a hoax if you ask me."

Sally Childs pulled back the microphone, then flickered a quick look at the camera man whose bushy eyebrows winged upward. "So, you think that nearly a hundred people dying in a matter of weeks is a hoax?"

The ruddy color in his face increased with his voice. "Yup. I don't know one person who's died from these so-called poison cigarettes." He pulled a cigarette pack from the worn pocket of his shirt and pointed to the camera before he lit one up and passed it to a red-haired man behind him. Ricky swooped in and collected his freebie, as the man lit another and passed it to a woman whose hand trembled as she tried to put a steady grip on it. "Had these all week. Nothing wrong with 'em." He lit another and put it to his lips, inhaling as he said. "Ain't nobody gonna stop me from smok–" The man collapsed as the crowd scattered in terror. Those with freshly lit cigarettes threw them to the ground, pensively waiting to see if they were next.

"Oh my God." Sally jumped back. "Sir? Sir?"

Jake noticed that the cameraman flinched, but managed to keep the camera rolling. He focused on the dying man for mere seconds before shifting to something more important coming down the street.

"Do you feel that?" Jake screamed to Ricky whose expression remained glued in shock. He snapped his fingers in front of his face and taunted, "Hello? Earth to Ricky."

"Huh?" He peeled his eyes from the twitching man, now surrounded by a stranger attempting CPR. "Feel what?"

The buzz of the crowd fizzled to a stir of whispers as the ground began to quake. One by one people scattered from the street as a line of military trucks rolled into town. Half raised signs teetered in the air as a booming voice came over a bullhorn. "By order of the United States Military this city is now under a mandatory quarantine. A city-wide curfew will begin this evening at nine o'clock and remain in effect until six o'clock tomorrow morning. All cigarettes, from all manufacturers including Zamka, will no longer be distributed or sold until further notice."

An uproar of objections sounded through the air as people hoisted their signs higher, screaming their frustrations to the passing trucks.

"We are actively investigating all possible sources of contamination and appreciate your cooperation."

Jake turned to Ricky and despite all the commotion around them, he smiled. "Come on, let's get out of here. You've been wondering what I've been up to. Now, I have something to show you."

CHAPTER 15

King of Wands

—◆··◆··◆—

Andi wrapped her scarf around everything except her eyes as she climbed through the hillside towards the old, abandoned church. The grey skies of winter complemented the tall black steeples that posed as crutches, holding up the deteriorating church. This was her sacred space, hidden away and forgotten by the rest of the world. A place that she visited every Sunday for hours of well-deserved alone time.

By the time Andi turned ten she had already lived in fifteen countries. The time she spent in each one was short, which made her list of friends even shorter. Despite the frequent uprooting which continued to dismantle her life, one thing remained the same. Every year, her parents would take her to the very place which inspired her name, The Andes Mountains. While her parents set off on the slopes, she would hike up the hill just far enough away from the lodge, sketchbook in hand, stenciling the vast and open snowscape. As her pages filled with repeated pines, and icy treasures, she realized that she still longed for more than what was before her. Her mind unwound upon the pages, forcing her hand to create the world she so deeply desired. Flipping through her journal you could see every version of home she had envisioned, every family supper she had mentally savored, and every friend she wished she'd had. The frigid winds of the winter slopes held no weight to her pencil. She would stay here for hours, until her fingers grew stiff and her cheeks were windswept to a nice shade of pink.

The day she stumbled upon the abandoned church, standing alone upon the snow-capped hill, long forgotten feelings emerged, and brought her back week after week.

She walked through the patches of grass and weeds peering up through the melting snow leading to the crumbled steps, and pulled out her sketchpad, wondering what aspect of the church she might recreate today. By now she had already drawn new steeples, a bell tower, and pages full of stained-glass. Restoring the place to what it had been when parishioners once graced its walls. Her hand hovered over the stark white paper as the wind howled through her thoughts. *You're all alone again.* She pressed the pencil firmly to the paper, attempting to combat her inner bully. *Kyle hasn't called because he's busy. Everything is fine.*

A noise came from within the church, just in time to halt her inner battle. An annoyed sigh slipped through her lips as she crept to the window and stood on her tiptoes, peeking through the fractured glass. The silhouettes of two males came into focus, one tall and lanky, the other scrawny and small. Around them was a typical array of supplies signifying squatters... sleeping bags, duffels, blankets, and... a mountainous stack of boxes.

Andi grabbed a hunk of rock from the stairs and returned to the window, standing on it to get a better look.

The tall lanky one paced between the boxes and the door, throwing his arms in the air as he yelled, "What do you mean you had a vision? You didn't even talk to me. Now all of our money is gone."

The other one interjected, "It's not gone. It's just ... invested in–"

"In cigarette patches?" The tall one took a swing at the stack of boxes sending them toppling to the floor. "Oh, sorry, not *all* of these are cigarette patches. You also bought all the rolling papers in town. What the fuck, Jake. How could you do this to us?"

"Ricky, I swear to God I was just setting up my stuff in the subway. All of the sudden it was like a movie just popped in my head and played out a memory that didn't belong to me."

The bigger one paced in front of the pulpit. "How long have you been stockpiling this stuff?" he looked back towards the impressive number of boxes. "Couldn't have done this all in one day?"

Jake nodded towards the confessional. "It took a few weeks; I hid them in there until I thought it was safe to tell you."

Ricky peered inside the empty confessional, as if some other prize might fall out. "Face it, you stopped telling me about your visions because you don't trust me with them."

Jake exhaled while tilting his head back, locking eyes with the painted angel overhead. "The last two times I told you about my visions you interfered with how they were supposed to play out. You took what was supposed to be for others, and... I just couldn't risk you doing that again."

Ricky thudded onto a pew as Jake walked the length of the aisle. "The food that I saw being tossed away in the alley was meant to feed the homeless kids... and as I went off to tell them, you went there and took what you wanted for yourself."

"I was hungry," Ricky asserted.

"You're always hungry." He snapped while turning to face him. "That food was meant for the kids."

Ricky's face twitched with judgement. "You act like you owe these kids something... you don't. They're just like you and me, out on the streets trying to stay alive. Look, you told them about this church and gave them somewhere to sleep every night, that's enough." He picked up a Bible and blew the dust off. "So, what, you trust me now?"

Jake sat down beside him. "I saw us, selling patches and loosies on the streets and making so much money. No more hungry nights, no more magic tricks, just–"

Ricky thumbed through the silky pages. "Just an opportunity to spend all our money?"

Jake angled towards him. "Because I know you, and you only want to live for the moment. This... took planning."

"Planning that you did without me." A weather-beaten top hat whipped off his head as he wiped the sweat from his forehead. "I gotta get out of here and get some air. I just can't talk to you right now."

Andi ducked from the window as Jake turned her way but not before he caught a glimpse of her eyes.

* * *

Jake moved a box to the window and stood on top of it, looking out to the cowering girl.

She cringed and rose to standing. "I was just out here getting some drawing done, and I thought I heard something," she said, her voice slightly panicked. The big almond eyes peering out at him from her scarf immediately disarmed him.

"Guess you were right." Jake teetered on the box, trying to get a better look at her. It was hard to tell what she looked like with her face concealed by layers of scarves, but from what he could see, she was enchanting.

"So, you're either trying to stop or start smoking... which is it?" She nodded towards the boxes piled up against the wall behind him.

Jake almost laughed at the humor in her tone, but remained warily cautious of the strange beauty. "I don't know yet."

She hopped down from the rock, slid passed the snow-covered stone bench, and entered the tall red doors of the church. "You know, if you'd wash that face of yours, you might actually be quite handsome. For a homeless guy."

"There's a compliment in there somewhere," he shot back, frowning. He'd once been considered the boy most likely to succeed, had been East Durham's most popular, so there might have been some truth in her words at one time. She, on the other hand, was absolutely beautiful. The kind of girl he would have met on the campus of some prestigious college, if his life had gone in that direction. "The name's Jake."

"Andi. When was the last time you were in public?" She rubbed her hands together, attempting to warm them. "I mean... do you know what's going on in town?"

"I heard there was a disease or something and figured I better stay up here for a bit. Not like I have anywhere else to be," Jake said, hoping she would buy it. He was always good at bending the truth for temporary gain. Something he learned from his father. Even in the years when he was certain he shared the same vision as his mother, his father found a way to discredit it. Looking back, he saw just how shrill his father had been.

Andi took a seat on the dusty pew and kicked her boots up. "I don't have a job right now either. The plant where I work was shut down." She put her focus on the boxes he'd accumulated. "New reports are saying that all of the deaths in town might be linked to the cigarettes we make."

"You don't say." Zamka, the place his father worked. That place that was the root cause of his mother's death, which he was beginning to question. He fished for more information on who this girl might be, and pulled a card from his bag, seeking some form of an answer.

Her gaze fell to the card and she frowned. "Yep. We're completely shut down. Cigarettes were pulled from the shelves. Now hundreds of people are out of jobs. We're not making them, and they're not smoking them."

Their gazes slowly lifted towards the heaps of patches.

Jake rubbed his fingers over the freshly drawn card, a symbol of a thick bellied Egyptian god with the wide eyes and bowed legs. He recalled its meaning, one which his mother taught him as a child. He could still hear her voice if he listened close enough. *Bes is a powerful deity, and protects all women and children. He is devoted to his purpose, yet full of joy and love. Hold this card close my dear.* He tucked the card away before Andi could inquire its meaning and returned his attention to the boxes.

"Odd coincidence that you happen to have those patches and papers over there." She unwound her scarf revealing even more of her face. "I think I can help you..."

Jake's gaze narrowed as he wondered what her motive could possibly be. Even he wasn't aware of how this would all play out. "Why should I trust you?"

"Because you need me to sell the rolling papers," she admitted, nodding in the direction of his private stash. "For the time being, I have access to loose tobacco that no one else has touched or tampered with."

Jake tried to hide his elation upon hearing those words. What were the odds of this stranger having the very thing that could make those particular items worthwhile? Supply and demand. Now he understood what the vision meant.

"I have keys to rooms and warehouses at Zamka that no one else does," she said, leaning against the old wooden lectern. "With my help, we can sell it all."

"We?" He looked to the door expecting Ricky to magically appear. Wouldn't be the case this time because he was truly angry. "What about my partner?"

She shrugged. "Do you want to split the money in half, or thirds?"

"Well, what I want to do and what I have to do is different."

Andi, pulled the scarf back around her face, walked towards the door and turned to him. "You know, if you're going to be selling to people in this town, you should probably look the part." She beckoned him with a mitten covered hand. "Come on, you can shower at my place."

CHAPTER 16

Knight of Swords

Fear spread through the news like wildfire, triggering panic, aggression, and a series of break-ins. Protests and rallies overtook the town, which was quickly crumbling to a jobless wasteland. All of this unrest was a journalist's perfect playground, a place where Sally Childs was certain she'd catch her next big break.

Sally stood outside of the local grocery store alongside the owner. The windows had been shattered for the third time that week. She looked toward the camera and took a breath. "Emotions are running deep today as Bill Myers, the owner of Durham Grocery, has a message for the town."

Despair and sadness settled in the man's dark brown eyes as he looked to Sally and held her gaze for a moment. "I have been in East Durham for sixty-five years, and not once has anything like this happened. These are my neighbors, my friends, breaking into my store. I...I just don't understand how this could happen."

Sally placed a comforting arm on his shoulder.

He looked to the camera to plead, "please, I know you are hurting right now, we all are, but it doesn't mean you can just break in and steal." His brow crinkled as he thought of one last thing. "You know what's odd to me? These people aren't after food... they're after something else that apparently, I don't have on the shelves. Please, whatever you're after, I don't have it."

* * *

Ricky pulled himself from the ground and staggered down the barren streets searching for Jake. The subway held no sign of him, nor did the steps outside of Zamka. He entered the woods and climbed the path towards the church where two voices echoed from within. He threw open the door as if he were a jilted lover bursting into a wedding, right at the moment the pastor said, "Speak now or forever hold your peace".

He gripped the doorframe for balance at the sight of the unfamiliar woman standing so close to Jake. "Who the fuck is this?" Ricky staggered down the aisle.

Jake looked to Andi and attempted to defuse the emerging argument. "She's here to help us."

Ricky snarled at Jake's freshly shaved face and swatted at his clean, new clothes. "I'm not talking about her."

"Sit down, let me explain."

"Fine." He took a seat on the floor near the boxes.

"This... is Andi. Andi worked for Zamka ... you know, the company that just got shut down."

"So." Ricky laid back on the ground, looking up to the rickety beams of the vaulted ceiling.

"So, she has access to lots of things by working there... including loose tobacco." He waited for any form of an 'ah-ha' moment. When one wasn't forthcoming he continued in a slow steady voice. "I bought all of the rolling papers and patches in town. With no shipments coming in or going out, we are now the sole suppliers of both cigarettes and patches."

If Ricky were a cartoon character, dollar signs would have appeared in his eyes as he sat up and answered, "We are?"

Andi gave a devilish smile. "What you see stacked alongside the rolling papers are two barrels full of loose tobacco. This is clean, fresh from the warehouse. Now, what do you say we get you cleaned up?"

Ricky glared at the newcomer, who had weaseled herself into their operation for two, and headed for the door. "We've always done things just you and me. We don't need anybody else. Never have."

Attempting to stop him from leaving, Jake insisted, "Remember my vision? All of our money is tied up in this stuff. She has access to tobacco and is the key to helping us sell it... you just need to look the part, that's all."

He paused in contemplation, as the thought of money outweighed his disdain for cleaning up for society. "Fine, but I'm not cutting my hair."

Together the three of them walked down the chaotic streets, taking in just how far the town had gone. The once clean, quiet, and crime free streets were now overrun with jobless, anxious people, all searching for relief in one form or another. Ricky and Jake spoke the language of addicts well, and could pinpoint every man, woman and child in need of what they had.

Ricky ran his fingers through his thick shiny hair and slid a pair of aviator glasses over his eyes. His long dark jacket coupled with his stark grey scarf gave off a GQ vibe as a few heads turned. Paying no mind to the act he hadn't experienced in years, he carried on down the wintery streets. "I think people are looking fatter. I mean, you can tell who has stopped smoking and who hasn't right? Look at that guy over there." He nodded towards a man shoveling chips in his mouth. "And what about that lady?" He looked at a woman nervously biting her nails as she waited for the bus. She could have been shaking from the winter chill, but odds were, it was something else.

Jake smirked, snagging a newspaper from a nearby park bench and scanning the pages. "Look at that ... DUI's up by fifty-five percent with domestic violence not far behind." He tossed it back down, but the wind whipped the pages away and down the street. "Seems people will find their coffin nails one way or another."

"Wanna see what they'd do for one? Watch this." Ricky removed one of his gloves and dug into his bag, pulling out a handful of freshly rolled cigarettes. "Loosies here," he yelled. "Clean, freshly rolled cigarettes, get em' here."

The shaky woman combed her bitten nails through the straggly curls of hair. "Hey," she said, avoiding eye contact. "I know this sounds crazy, but man... I really need one." Her watery blue eyes narrowed to slits. "These are all clean? How do you know?"

Andi interjected, "We have access to tobacco from a farm outside of town. If you don't believe us, we'll smoke one right here."

"Do you mind?" She glanced over her shoulder then back at him. "I'd feel better just making sure... you know?"

Ricky placed the cigarette to his lips, inhaling the sweet taste of money. "See," he said, exhaling a cloud of smoke in her face, "clean as a whistle."

"Oh, thank you." She threw her arms up, trying to hug him but he stepped off to the side and she missed. She mumbled something and returned to her seat.

"Hey, remember that guy in the train station that offered me money to put the card in his gift box?"

Ricky tucked the smokes back into the bag. "Yeah."

"I keep seeing him and another man," he said, twisting to check behind them. "I swear they're following me."

Ricky scanned the near empty streets, finding only a few folks still out and about. "Well, if he was, you'd be able to spot him." He checked his watch. "Curfew isn't for two more hours, wonder where everybody is?"

Jake looked over his shoulder once more. "When we were down and out, where did we like to go?"

Ricky flicked his gaze between the closest bar and the strip club.

Andi interrupted their banter. "You know, we should be careful about how we sell these. We can't just do it out in broad daylight like this." She nodded towards the neon glow of the flashing pink donkey. "Come on, I have an idea."

"Maybe I do like this girl." Ricky playfully elbowed Jake's side.

"Told you," Jake said with a boyish grin as they entered the dimly lit lounge packed full of people. "So, this is where everyone has run off to," Jake mumbled under his breath.

Ricky posted up at the bar, admiring the green-haired girl with thick eyeliner and pink lashes. Her lips were cherry red, her spiky heels tall and black.

"What can I get ya?" she leaned across the bar, pushing her breasts up even further.

"Whisky and a dance?" Ricky stared at the garter belt peeking through her ripped fishnets as she twirled towards the bottles. She winked while sliding the glass across the bar. "This one's on me."

"Thanks ..."

"Candy," she said, licking her lips.

"And the dance..."

"Oh... well, we only got one dancer right now, so it might be a minute. Oh, look at that," she nodded towards a group of men staggering from a table near the stage. "If you hurry you can snag that booth over there. Now, which one of you is getting the dance?"

Andi slid a credit card onto the bar. "The dance is actually for all three of us."

Candy didn't blink an eye at the request. "You got it. Jade will be with ya when she can."

They settled into the U-shaped pleather booth, cracked and worn from years of pleasure seekers, and turned their focus to the curvaceous vixen on the stage. Her long platinum hair fell past her waist, as she kept her back to them, slowly removing her clothing piece by piece between gyrations. Ricky's wide eyes followed her across the stage, watching as she slid her legs around the pole and climbed to the top. He mindlessly threw dollars upon the stage, as she hung upside down, suddenly revealing a huge pregnant belly.

"Oh God," he gasped, inching backward. "I don't know if I should throw more money or..."

"Stop it," Jake scolded, "At least stay until she's done."

She crawled across the stage towards them, stuffing the money wherever it would fit. "Something the matter boys?"

"No, I mean, you sure you should be dancing or ...?" Ricky blurted out as she slid from the stage onto his lap.

"Now if you don't want the dance," she purred. "There's a lot of other men here that do."

Ricky parted his lips to speak.

"Jade is it?" Andi interrupted before Ricky could make a mess of things.

She moved on top of Andi, rolling her hips while whispering in her ear, "it's whatever you want it to be." She slid her hand between Andi's thighs and eased them open. Andi tilted her chin just inches from Jade's lips as she clamped her knees closed. "I appreciate the offer, but I have one better for you."

Jade bit her pouty lip in a half-offended, half turned-on way.

"You see, we—meaning us three here," Andi glanced towards her comrades. "Have come to possess a great deal of product that..."

"What kind of product?" Jade said, her gaze narrowing with suspicion. "They've got enough drugs running through here. That's not what people are looking for right now."

"Clean tobacco and cigarette patches," Andi said, ignoring Ricky's glare.

Those words made her pause and give them a second look. Now we can't just be selling these on the streets... and are looking for a... partner."

Jade slowed her hips to a near stop and sat back. "Would I be just your partner, or them too?"

Andi looked to Jake and Ricky for approval, they both nodded, and she answered, "Split four ways."

Jade ran her fingers down her stomach and reached into her silky red thong, extracting a business card.

Andi gave a half-smile half-cringe as she accepted the damp card in her hands.

"Bring your product by tomorrow, and I'll get to work."

CHAPTER 17

The Fool

A knock came at the door interrupting the latest news story. Ben got up from the loveseat. "I'll get it."

Maggie quieted the television, which meant she was attempting to listen from the den.

"Hey Ben, sorry to bother you this time of night." Luther glanced over Ben's shoulder. "Mind if I come in?"

"Sure, what can I do for you?"

Maggie inched down the hallway at the same moment Luther leaned against the door.

"A young man named Kyle McGinnis hasn't been seen for a few days. We're asking folks that might have known him a few questions."

"That's a shame about the boy; sorry to say I haven't seen him."

"I'm actually here to talk to Tristan. Is he here?" Luther angled so he could see up the stairs.

"Oh, uh, yes let me ..." He paused as Tristan trudged down the stairs. "Speak of the devil."

"Hey Luther, is this about Summer?" A hint of hope cracked through his voice.

"Sorry Tristan, no." Luther scratched his head, grimacing as though he hadn't expected that question. "I'm actually here to talk about Kyle McGinnis, did you know him well?"

He gripped the banister, frowning as his foot halted in mid-step. "What do you mean 'did'?

"Sorry. Do you know him?"

Tristan walked down a few more steps. "What's this about? Is he okay?"

"He hasn't been seen for a couple of days. We're trying to determine his whereabouts. When was the last time you saw him?" Luther pressed his pen to paper awaiting an answer.

Ben's face remained devoid of emotion as he thought of the last text message Tom had sent, which was a picture of Kyle's Jeep with the words 'it is done.' He shifted his stance, acting as if he were listening to Luther, but continued mauling over his recent actions. *Did I delete that text?*

"Couple weeks ago." Tristan answered. "We met at the coffee shop to study. We were there about two hours and then Kyle said he had something to do. I'm not–"

"Maggie, why don't you get Officer Cooper something to drink."

She scurried into the kitchen, calling over her shoulder as she rustled through the refrigerator. "Luther, what can I get you? Iced tea? Coffee? Soda?"

"Thank you, Maggie, but I'm just fine."

Not minding his instructions, she began pulling out a few select times. "You sure?"

"Yes ma'am," he smiled at her constant hospitality. "Sorry, where were we?"

"You were asking me about Kyle... he didn't tell me where he was going but I don't think he would have gone far; he had a big project that was due in the lab this week."

"And what was his area of study?"

"Bio molecular engineering."

Luther seemed to stumble over writing that one. "Did he have any conflicts at school or at home that you know of?"

Tristan shook his head then smiled. "Does liking a girl that is too smart for you count?"

Luther lifted his pen from the page. "And this girl?"

Maggie butted into their conversation, announcing a platter of meat and cheese. "Now, I know you must be hungry. Come on, eat up."

While his hands were occupied, Tristan slid a glance towards Ben, unable to decipher the warning glare about sharing too much.

"She's a friend of ours," Tristan admitted, putting his focus on Luther again. "Her name is Andi."

Maggie thrust a napkin in his hands. "There you go."

"Okay, well I appreciate your time tonight," he said around a mouthful of food. "Umph, this is good." He inhaled, straightened his shoulders, and grabbed up a few more of the offering into a napkin to go. "I'm sure Kyle will turn up soon. Most cases like this, the person just went on a road trip and didn't tell anybody." He polished off the last bite, then tipped his hat towards Maggie. "Thank you for your hospitality, pleasure as always."

She opened the door, as he nodded and said, "Ben."

"Luther."

As the door closed behind him all eyes turned to Tristan who was brimming with questions. "What do you know about Kyle?" His gaze and tone were both accusatory. "And don't lie either, I know he was here. I saw his jeep pull out of the driveway the other night."

Ben tried to keep his expression neutral. "There are some things better left unspoken." He headed back towards the den, skirting the question and his wife.

Agitated, Tristan followed. "My friend is missing, and I think that warrants a conversation, don't you? Mom?" He called behind him down the empty hallway with Maggie fresh on his heels.

Ben relaxed into his reclining chair and reached for this favorite book. "Look Tristan, I'm sure wherever he is, he has good reason being there. Don't exhaust yourself looking for him. I'm sure he'll turn up."

Tristan's face remained twisted in confusion. "And if he doesn't?"

Ben's finger slid between the pages, picking up where he left off. "You carry on."

Tristan disappeared into the shadows of the hallway, sulking towards his bedroom, as a sudden vibration came from the seat cushion. Puzzled, Ben looked at his silent phone, then scrambled for the flip phone tucked in his back pocket to read the incoming text

Have you been going to see her?

Ben tamped down on the surge of anger that swept through him, dialed and scolded in a hushed whisper, "I thought I told you not to text me."

"I'm sorry, Ben," the voice on the other end said. "But there's a problem."

"Oh yeah? No shit." Ben leaned from the chair, inching toward the entrance to ensure the hallway was empty before continuing. "What the heck happened with the packages? Do you know what your carelessness has done?"

"What?" Silence hung on the line for a few moments. "I don't know what you're talking about. I did exactly what you..."

"Then what problem are you talking about?" Ben asked between clenched teeth.

"I got a call from the care center," he said. "They're starting to ask questions about how I'm paying and the way I'm paying it. You know, a truck driver's salary paying that much in cash, doesn't add up."

Ben thought that over for a moment, wondering if somehow the payments could be traced. "Trust me, everything is fine. Continue to do as I ask, and the payments will continue to come."

"That isn't all. The last package... the locker was empty."

He growled into the phone, "What do you mean it was…" He paused. "Repeat the code."

"1, 24, 37, 73." He waited, "Sir?"

"Was there anything out of the ordinary when you went this time?"

A low throaty chuckle echoed from the other end. "Yeah, a woman went into labor, nearly knocked me over when she screamed."

"And this woman, did she go into labor before or after you checked the locker?"

"Before. Oh, and the locker wasn't completely empty," he said. "There was a pocket watch inside."

Pocket watch. "The woman, did you see anybody with her?" Ben gripped the phone so tight his knuckles ached.

"Uh… yeah actually, it was a man: tall, blue eyes, trench coat and a top hat."

The image of a worn-out top hat came to mind. "I'll be in touch." Ben tucked the phone back into his pocket and resumed reading a passage from his favorite book. This was something he had read time and time again, to remind him that humans aren't the only ones that use others to avoid being captured.

"And when the starling sensed it was being hunted by the hawk, it took to the sky and began its dance. The others observed his pattern of distress and joined him. Before long, thousands of birds concealed the one, silently moving together like a symphony orchestrated by an unseen hand. Together they danced through the sky, twisting in ribbons, and expanding into a cloud of dazzling darkness. But where has the starling gone? He has left the dance and returned to the trees, where he watches Mother Nature's greatest trick from afar."

"Honey?" Maggie leaned her head in the room. "Sorry, I know you're reading, but there's something I think you need to see." She flipped on the television and turned to the local news.

He put the book aside and together they watched live serial footage of cigarette manufacturing facilities across the country being raided. A ribbon spanned the bottom of the screen, "Up in Smoke: Cigarette Plants under Fire."

Ben could practically feel her anxiety sucking every ounce of air out of the room. "Now it's all the cigarette companies."

"Until they figure things out, I guess that's what has to be done." He slid the book back into his hands and put his focus on the pages again.

Her eyes widened with shock. "That's your answer? What are we supposed to do to support our family? Sell the farm?" She waited in vain for any form of acknowledgment before leaving the room. "I'm going to bed."

Ben huffed, repositioning himself to look at the framed watercolor painting on the wall of a duck and ducklings crossing a street. Behind the simple painting, a dormant memory laid covered, but if he stared at it long enough, he could still see the outline of Iris' face. Truth of it was, he had sold the farm, which accounted for the very large sum of money now sitting in their bank account. Money that would take him far away from here when the time was right. He'd let the lawyers sort out everything with Maggie.

He folded his hands over his chest and exhaled, recalling the walk home from his first date with Iris. *Fall had arrived, and she had on a bright red coat and lipstick to match; her short blonde hair in uneven pigtails, and loud chunky heels clanked upon the pavement.*

"You look upset," he said as she dug in her purse for another cigarette.

Her beautiful smile made up for the foul words that often came from it. "You wouldn't understand...I just need this right now." She lit her next cigarette off the last and looked away.

"Whatever it is you're going through, I promise, I can help."

She exhaled a cloud of smoke to the autumn air, finding temporary relief. "Until you see the world like I do, you can't."

Something irked him as he tumbled through his memories of Iris and beckoned him.

He looked at his watch, weighing his need for sleep against getting answers, before springing for the door. He wheeled his bike to the edge of the drive, kicking the mud from his boots before getting on. The moon illuminated the country road as he headed east towards the forest, where towering pines would guide him the rest of the way.

In the distance, the warm lights of a luxury care center peered through the trees, signaling his next turn into a more secluded part of the woods. He parked his bike and walked the trail towards the back entry; swapped his old shirt for something newer, scanned the keycard hanging around his neck, and slid inside. The halls were quiet; except for the sound of late-night television shows coming from a few occupied rooms. Ben bypassed the yoga studio, art room, and spa, creeping towards the last room on the right, where a dim light shone beneath the door. He had exactly four minutes until the nightly guard would make his rounds, which meant he had to hurry.

Inside, she laid still and fragile, hooked up to ventilators like a fallen marionette. The cold metal rails of her bed eased his sweating palms as he stood there beside her.

"Oh Iris," he whispered, closing his eyes. "I'm glad you finally get to enjoy the silence you so deeply deserve—no voices, no visions, just peace. I know you didn't have anywhere to turn back then, and maybe I should have done better, but…" He scanned the empty room. "I'm changing things… you wouldn't believe it… not exactly in the way I envisioned, but those people are going to get what they deserve."

He leaned in with a joyous whisper, "Oh, and guess what? I sold the farm. I bet you never thought that day would come." He squeezed her hand and gave a few departing words. "Just know that when you wake up, the world will look so much different and we'll be happy again."

Ben wasn't a believer in her art, but with the way things had unfolded, he certainly believed now.

CHAPTER 18

Knight of Pentacles

Luther stared at six pictures of the recently deceased scattered across his desk, massaging his temples in frustration as the last of the lights went out in the precinct. By this time all the others had gone home to their families, while he chose to stay in the place that housed his greatest achievements, as well as his greatest downfalls. He averted his eyes from the victims, their faces interchangeable in his troubled mind with six others from his past, and looked towards the framed picture of his two boys sitting on his desk.

If he looked close enough, he could still read the note written on the back of the picture. A note that arrived on his desk days before the trial, outlining exactly how he was to comply, and how the verdict was to be rendered, which included a settlement in the amount of 3.6 million dollars to be awarded to the victim's families, and a very large sum of money for himself.

He closed his eyes, as the ghastly scene ripped through his memory.

The rain seemed to blow in sideways that day, typical for a summer afternoon in the South. Through the pouring rain, cries of despair carried from the field, as he followed Iris' voice. He found her on her knees, sobbing over the body of a lifeless child. Her once white dress was covered in mud, and stuck to her quivering body as she pointed from one child to the next. "I just... found them out here, on the ground, not moving. All of them. Oh God."

Luther made a quick assessment of the scene. Work clothes. Tools in hand. Not one of them over the age of twelve.

"Where's Ben?"

"Uh," she wiped the rain from her face and scanned the field, looking as perplexed as he did. "He was just right here, he must have run back to the house, maybe to get help?"

Before he could help her to standing, a fleet of black cars arrived, armed with suited men eager to seize the fields. One of them bumped Luther's shoulder while muscling through, nearly knocking him over.

"Hey now, wait just one minute, this is a crime scene here. Who are you people?" Luther paced behind the giant, suited men as one spoke up for the group. "This is a federal investigation. Your assistance is no longer needed here." The two tallest ones stood shoulder to shoulder obstructing his view while the others draped black tarps over the bodies.

"But..." he looked to Iris who couldn't manage to peel her eyes from the twisted operation.

The agent took another step towards him. "I said, you're no longer needed sir."

Luther wrapped his arm around Iris as they headed back towards the house.

"Don't worry Iris, I promise I'll get to the bottom of this."

Money tips the scales of justice time and time again. For Luther, who was a widowed father of two, it didn't take much. Just two college funds and a promise that his boys would always remain unharmed. The framed reminder of his ability to be bought remained on his desk, staring him in the face if ever he chose to question his morals again.

With Zamka Tobacco back in the headlines, this was his chance for redemption. Sure, there were plenty of other officers who could work this case, but to him it was personal.

He returned his attention to the faces of the victims, reached into the cold metal drawers of his desk, and pulled out a stack of colorful notecards, thread, and pushpins. With an invigorated heave he sprung from the chair and headed towards the cork board, an old friend he hadn't visited with in years.

He looked to his hand of victims, pulling out the one that still had a chance of being alive, Kyle McGinnis. Below his image were the names of a similar crowd, including best friend Tristan Flowers, alleged girlfriend Andi Stephens, employer Zamka Tobacco, and a card that noted 'family-diseased.'

He cringed at the third image, the man from the motel fire, and pinned his picture to the wall. He paused, remembering the set of prints they had pulled from the Lysol can, and went charging back to his desk. As he clicked through the findings his breath slowed, as if attempting to prepare his mind for what he was reading. Confirmed prints belonged to Gina Stockton, wife of the CEO of Zamka Tobacco, Sam Stockton.

He hurried back to the board, added a new card for her, then took a step back. His attention fixated on the common threads: Zamka Tobacco, Tristan Flowers, and Andi Stephens.

He tilted his head, studying each one. *Sure, Zamka had high paying attorneys and a slew of shady goons to cover their dirty work, but they wouldn't destroy their own brand.* He plucked the card from the wall labelled Zamka and moved to the next.

Tristan Flowers was a good, straight-laced kid. The type of kid that didn't have rhyme or reason to destroy the very thing that put food on his table and a roof over his head.

The last card on the wall glared back at him as a buzz came from his pocket, causing him to jump. He pulled the cellphone from his pants and crinkled his nose at the Caller ID that read, 'do not answer.' He picked up the phone and sat in silence. She didn't deserve a 'hello,' she barely deserved the last goodbye he gave her.

"Luther? You there?" Sally asked in that innocent tone that no longer fooled him.

An exaggerated sigh preceded his words. "What do you want Sally?"

"You know I wouldn't call you if it wasn't serious, but... I received a threat."

Her words caused him to sit up a little straighter. "What kind of threat?"

Her voice was hesitant as she pulled the words from her lips. "One like you got... fifteen years ago."

The younger version of Luther would have asked where she was and rushed to her aid, but the older, wiser version said, "Tell me more."

"I found a knife stabbed into my front door, with a thumb drive taped to the handle. There were images on it... of you and me, from years ago. Images I didn't even know existed.

Us arguing outside the morgue, and other... more intimate ones.”

“Last I checked, dating isn’t a crime.” He turned his attention back to his computer where the bio of Andi Stephens was displayed. He wasn’t giving Sally his full attention, even if her story warranted it.

“Whoever these people are, they know about us...which means they know about what really happened. Look, I’m calling you because if they could cover up the deaths of innocent children, then they won’t blink an eye when it’s our turn.”

He paused in silence, homing in on the two words that sparked his interest, ‘parents deceased’.

“You know what, this was a mistake calling you. Just forget it.”

“Wait...” he intercepted, kicking himself for the words that would follow. “Where are you?”

CHAPTER 19

The Stars

Ben rolled over, coming face to face with the open mouth beside him hissing like a stuffed exhaust pipe. As though sensing his presence, Maggie snorted herself awake.

"Good morning." She rubbed her eyes and grabbed his hands. "Didn't hear you come to bed last night, were you up late?"

"Not too late."

She snuggled closer. "Where'd you go?"

"Far enough to clear my mind."

Maggie looked towards the clock as he pulled himself from bed. "And how does it feel to sleep in like a normal person?"

Normal person? Yes, he took her meaning, but still, did she have to voice it that way? "Doesn't feel right," he answered.

"Well, when all of these things are resolved, everything will be back to normal in no time. Bet you're glad you cashed in..." She quickly covered her words with a smile. "Never mind."

Her eyes remained glued to the wall as her mind jumped to a new topic. "What do you think about painting the bedroom yellow? You know, like a soft buttercup?"

He nodded, knowing that it would never happen. "Mmm hmm. Going to head downstairs and grab the paper." The moment he opened the door he came face to face with two men in black suits. They had the demeanor of federal agents, and certainly didn't fit the description of small-town cops.

The taller of the two presented a badge. "Ben Flowers?"

"Yes," he slowly picked up the paper before one of them crushed it under his shiny loafer. Maggie's footsteps tipped back.

"ATF, can we come in?"

"Of course." He stepped aside as they entered the kitchen.

"I'm sure it's no secret what we're here to talk to you about." They paced the kitchen like they owned the place, scowling at the simplest of things. Even the bowl of fruit seemed to be under scrutiny. "So we'll just get right to it. Ben, how long have you known Sam Stockton?"

Before answering he called to the other room, "Maggie, make sure you're decent. We have visitors." As if she didn't already know that. He paused, listening for that shuffle to take her back up the stairs.

"Well, Sam and I have known each other since we were kids, being cousins and all. The family farm is the backbone of our business, which he always had a better knack for running. My collar is a bit too blue to work alongside him, if you know what I mean."

"And how was business, before the recent events?"

"Sam and I stayed in our lanes." He picked up an apple and shined it on his sleeve. "I was good with the farming and he was good with... everything else. Neither one of us dabbled in each other's business."

The two men shared a glance. Agent Willow leaned in to whisper to Agent Stone, before he said, "We have records of you coming into the city for several meetings with Sam recently. Can you tell us what those were about?"

He folded his arms across his chest, wondering if he could share such private information with anyone outside of the company. He embellished on what tidbits he could. "Some silly idea involving trends I'm too old to understand. The kids in my lab latched onto the idea though, seems they know so much more than me these days."

"And these kids in your lab... was one of them Kyle McGinnis?"

"Uh, yes. But due to recent events we have cancelled labs, so I'm not sure how much progress they have made on the project."

"They," one of the agents hedged.

"Andi."

Agent Stone's head whipped up. "Andi Stephens?"

"Yes, I believe that is her last name," Ben said, wondering why that bit of information brought such a response. "Really bright girl. To be honest, I think Kyle is a little jealous of her, but I shouldn't be telling their private business."

The taller man cocked his head while scribbling notes. "Their business? Are they a couple?"

"I can only speculate that they are," he said with a chuckle. "That boy follows her like a sad puppy."

"Interesting," Agent Willow said with another look to his partner. "Do you have any reason to believe that your products could have been tampered with?"

"I work the night shift, and only see what goes on during those hours," he said, trying to ascertain what information to share to throw them off his scent. Something other than, "I guess it's possible that someone could have tried to alter the products, but I gave all of that data to Sam, so he has it."

"And what data was that?"

What they wanted to hear was—ratios, packaging dates, shipments, and a few other things. I just pulled the reports down off the machines and gave it to him on a thumb drive. Instead, he said, "Data he requested. Information on our machines back up nightly to tapes that Linda takes home."

The pencil stopped moving across the pad. "Wait, did you say that all of your proprietary data is backed up on tapes and stored at someone's house?" His gaze locked in on Ben.

"That's just how we've always done it."

"Thank you, Ben," he said, a sudden urgency in his words and movements. "You've been very helpful."

He followed them to the door, silently assessing their rush to pick up the lead he'd dropped. "I hope you don't mind me asking, but do you have any idea what is causing this? I know you aren't allowed to share information with the public, but this is my family business and I'm really worried here..."

They exchanged hesitant glances before the taller one leaned in to whisper, "What we tell you needs to be kept private."

"I understand."

"And if we find out that you've shared this information or interfered with the investigation in any way, we will come back and charge you."

He nodded. "Of course."

"We have found traces of Teflon in a substantial amount of cigarettes specifically tied to brands that your company manufactures," he said as his partner focused on Ben, probably hoping for some sort of reaction. "At this time, there are a lot of unknowns and inconsistencies but that's what we know."

As they sped off in their oversized car, Ben grabbed his keys off the nail in the wall, calling up the stairs, "Be back in a few". Once on the highway, his cycle roared as he opened the throttle, speeding towards the city.

The morning bustle of East Durham slowed Ben's progress as he combed every street, alley, and corner until at last he found Ricky, sitting alone in a fancy bistro in a booth by the window.

Ben plucked a menu from the podium and took the seat across from the kid, whose eyes were glued to his phone. The words "Ain't nobody gonna stop me from smok..." triggered laughter as the video replayed again and again.

"Ah hem," Ben coughed, forcing Ricky's attention his way.

He brushed his long hair from his shaven face and eyed the lowly farmer. "I'm sorry man, do I know you?"

Ben signaled the waitress for coffee, agitating Ricky further. "Look, I'm trying to enjoy a meal here. If you want them, they're $100 a pack, take it or leave it."

Ben placed the menu on the table next to the salt and pepper shakers, trying to process the words the boy had thrown out. "Say that again?"

"I said, they're $100 a pack; that is what you're here for right?" He refilled his cup of coffee with the French Press on the table and stirred in a dainty cube of sugar.

Ben remained silent as Ricky continued, "We have patches too, if that's what you're after. Same price."

The waitress slid an omelet, toast, and an assortment of jellies in front of Ricky and turned to Ben.

"You ready?" she said, her feet tapping an impatient rhythm against the tiles.

"Just coffee for me." Her hands shook as she poured, spilling coffee to the table. Ben waved off her attempts to clean it up. "Now, you were saying–"

"I was saying do you fucking want cigarettes or patches?" Ricky answered with his mouth full of food.

Cigarettes or patches. Just as he thought. Black market items now that Zamka had shut down and no one could get them within a hundred-mile radius of East Durham. Ben leaned over the table with an excited whisper. "Let me tell you why I'm here. Soon, a company is going to invent a device that can check cigarettes for poison. Once this machine hits the market, you and your friend will no longer be in business. But ... I will give you ten grand if you do me a favor."

Chunks of egg filled the gaps in his smile. "You've got my attention."

"Deliver the contents of the blue envelope to the name at this address, and the manila one leave at reception at this address here." He placed two post-it notes upon the table. It is important that the contents of the blue envelope be hand delivered to the man's office without his knowledge. Do you understand?"

Ricky scanned the surrounding faces, wondering who, if anyone might be listening. "That's it? Just hide whatever's in that envelope in someone's office, and leave the other one at a desk?"

"That's it."

Ricky's gaze narrowed on him. "I don't know you. How will I get my money?"

"You already have it. Well, some of it. The duffle bag that was in the locker... there was a code inside. Did you find it?"

"I don't know what you're talking about," he replied, his gaze sliding to the window.

Ben stood and moved away from the table. "Well that's too bad, I must have the wrong kid." He made it halfway to the door before Ricky blurted out, "wait."

Ben returned to his seat with a gleam of triumph in his eyes. Ricky checked the crowd once more and lowered his voice. "Jake handles the money now. I didn't get to look in the bag."

Ben took another sip of coffee before answering. "Well, half of the money is in the duffle bag, as well as a code that unlocks the next locker where you will find the rest. Once the job is done, meet me in the subway, 6 p.m. sharp, and I will give you a train ticket leading you to the next locker. Once you're out of town, I'll need you to stay there for at least a few months."

Ricky tossed a wrinkled twenty on the table, swiped up both envelopes, and headed for the door.

* * *

The smell of rain permeated the air as herds of people flooded the subway, shaking off their clothes and umbrellas as they entered. Ben waited patiently near the turnstile, scanning the crowd for his messenger. He smiled, admiring the man whose soul had been hardened by years of failure, a man unmoved by a thing as simple and wonderful as rain. His waterlogged trench coat dragged behind him as he flicked a cigarette to the ground, spotting the old man in the corner.

Ben pulled the ticket from his pocket as Ricky approached. "Is it done?"

"Yup."

Sensing something amiss he scanned the crowd, catching a glimpse of a pregnant woman leaning against the lockers.

"Should I have bought two tickets?"

"What?" Ricky fidgeted. "Look man, I did what you asked. The contents of the blue envelope are in that guy's office, and the other one is at the desk."

Ben yanked back the ticket. "Describe his office."

Ricky sighed before putting his focus on the pregnant woman, nodding for her to come. She smacked gum as she trounced towards them. Ricky whispered into her ear, and she answered for him. "Nice place. Fancy leather chairs... big *wood* desk." She squeezed Ricky's butt while blowing out an unladylike bubble. "Would have liked to help myself to that liquor too... but..." She winked and rubbed her belly.

Ben extended the ticket. "Where did you hide it?"

"The package in the cabinet behind the scotch ... like the note said."

He tucked the ticket into her palm, relieved that they had actually come through. "Thank you."

Ricky wrapped his arm around her, shielding her from further interaction. "Come on, let's go."

"Nice doing business with you." Ben smirked before fading back into the crowd. He dipped into the alleyway, heading towards his bike as his phone vibrated. Their words, though concealed by the privacy of raindrops, echoed in his mind like a siren whirling his guilt to the world.

"Hello?"

"Ben, it's Officer Cooper."

Silence lingered as he questioned, "You there?"

"Sorry Luther, must have hit a dead spot." His feet locked to the pavement, bracing himself.

"Need to talk to you about Kyle McGinnis."

Ben closed his eyes as the rain poured down. *Kyle again.*

Luther stepped into the alley, walking towards him as he lowered his phone. "You got some explaining to do, Ben," he said, holding a pack of cigarettes up in the air. "You know where I found these? On the body of Kyle McGinnis. You know Kyle McGinnis, don't you? Worked in your lab?"

"Boy was a smoker and worked at a cigarette company," Ben said, shrugging. "Nothing strange about that."

Luther's icy glare sent chills down his spine. "What's strange is the playing card cigarette we found on the body, the Queen of Hearts, contaminated with traces of poison."

Ben inhaled, tried to shake some of the guilt from his conscience. "Whatever he was doing in the lab while I wasn't there... I have no knowledge of that. Like I told the ATF earlier today, the boy was fascinated with addiction."

Nearly nose-to-nose Luther tilted his head. "ATF came looking?"

He nodded, wondering why it was a shock. "They were asking about Sam and the college kids I have working in the lab. Trust me Luther, my family's blood, sweat, and tears are in that land, and I wouldn't do anything to put that in jeopardy. The design for the playing card cigarettes... those came from Sam and Pete. I wasn't even involved in that decision."

Luther took a step backwards. "Don't you want to know where we found Kyle's body?"

"Never had a strong stomach," he answered. "Best keep that to yourself."

"Backwoods, sitting upright in the driver's seat of his Jeep holding a half-lit cigarette. What's got me troubled are the rope burns around his ankles and the cuts on his back... almost like someone dragged him there."

Ben shrugged as the phone in his back pocket vibrated. "Never know what things people are into. I'll keep his family in my prayers."

"His family is dead Ben. Lots of people in this town are." Luther took a few steps back as a call came in over the radio. "This conversation isn't over. Until next time..."

As Ben raced for home, a silent battle tore through his mind. Too many people were getting dangerously close to his secrets. He thought back to the card reading, recalling Iris' words 'the ends justify the means.' *Was she somehow justifying what was sure to come next?*

Ben pulled into the driveway then slid into the secrecy of his office, checking the hallway before dialing.

"Hey," Ben scolded. "Stop texting me."

"Well, you're behind on your payments."

"You don't think I know that?" Ben growled, unable to raise his voice. "Just do me a favor and stop texting me."

"Fine, but when are you going to settle up?"

"There's one last thing I need you to do for me."

The silence on the other end was a little disconcerting. Ben had never been late before and each new job seemed increasingly more risky.

Ben massaged his temple as he inched the words from his lips. "Do this and I'll pay you two-fold."

"What then?"

As if avoiding the inevitable instructions, Ben laid out a scenario he believed would bring his point home. "Have you ever seen a starling outsmart a hawk? Brilliant thing it is to watch. When that seemingly feeble bird senses trouble, it takes to the sky erupting in a dance of sorts. The patterns of distress signals for the others to join. Soon, thousands of birds sway in a melodramatic dance across the sky, concealing the one, as the hunter flies away. Though, it seems this time the hawk has learned the patterns of deception and waits for the starling to settle in the trees."

By now the man on the other end was used to Ben's parables. "And this hawk?"

"Cooper's Hawk. Soars at night. I'm going to text you the name of a computer genius, someone who can hack into his patrol car; once I send you the text delete it okay?"

"Alright. What do you want this hacker to do?"

Ben mulled over the next plan. "Have her radio car 57 once you get to your desired location, then the rest is up to you."

"Why would this hacker agree to do that? Are you paying her too?"

"Send her this picture and tell her that unless she complies, footage will surface of her creating poison cigarettes. When it's done, discard your phone and call me from the next train station."

The man paused to check the incoming message. "What's this picture ... a Queen of Hearts?"

Ben quickly disconnected, sensing a shadow lurking in the doorway behind him.

"Who were you talking to?" Maggie asked, frowning as she inched into the room.

"An old friend."

"You've been gone nearly half the day; where've you been?"

"Went into town, had to take care of a few things."

She sighed and a world of disappointment settled in that sound. "You've been disappearing an awful lot lately. Is everything okay Ben?"

He left his office and peered down the hallway. "Come in here, close the door. We need to talk."

"Yes, we do need to talk." Her unusually stern voice silenced him. "Tristan isn't doing well. He hasn't come out of his room in days, and won't eat. I'm worried he's shutting the world out."

"Everyone grieves in different ways."

"Come on Ben, could you at least act like you care?"

"I care about my son," Ben countered, angered that she would say such a thing.

She placed her hands to her hips. "Oh yeah, and just how is your son doing? You know, the one from your previous marriage that I never knew existed until recently.

Ben wrapped her hands in his. "It's not worth discussing."

"I think it is." She snatched her hands away. "What happened Ben? Just come clean for God's sake."

"You really want to know?" he yelled, tired of her endless questions. "My previous wife went insane, okay. She heard voices, claimed she saw spirits, and it drove her mad. She couldn't keep her thoughts straight, and swore she was being haunted by the ghosts of six children. She even tried to burn down the family farm; said the voices would go away if she could make it all stop."

Maggie's face softened under the weight of his confession. "I'm so sorry Ben. What happened to her?"

The image of Jake bursting through the door as Iris was carted off came to mind. If he would have arrived home just three minutes earlier he would have been able to say goodbye, but those were three minutes Ben didn't want to endure.

"I had her committed. As much as I hated doing it, I just couldn't stand to see her wither away into madness. Ironically, the only way she seemed to be able to cope with the visions was to smoke." He grimaced, hating that he had to relive this painful part of his life. "The COHb in her body had reached such toxic levels that it was too late. She slipped into a coma and ... died."

Hopefully, this greatly altered version of the truth would suffice, because it's all he cared to tell her. He left out the crucial parts involving the bodies she had found, and the public shaming she underwent at the trial that pushed her to the breaking point.

"And Jake?"

"Disapproved of my decision," he answered. "Said he'd rather live on the streets than eat at my table."

Maggie turned her back to him. "You could have told me; you know that's what partners are for. Now, what did you want to talk about?"

Before Ben had met Maggie, he had admired her work from afar. She was what they referred to as an emerging scientist in the field of chemical development. While she was responsible for inventing the heat sensitive ink that Ben eventually came to possess, her most prized creation was a sensory tool that detected and defined chemicals, all with one simple scan. One might compare it to a pregnancy test, but for elements instead. The once fast paced, meticulous scientist forfeited her dreams the day she met Ben. He had buried that guilt a long time ago, but now it called him from the grave.

"Do you remember that convention?" His eyes narrowed on her. "You know, the one in Dallas?" He thought back to the moment he first laid eyes on her, standing up on the stage looking out to the crowd from the podium.

Her cheeks flushed as she answered, "How could I forget. You stared at me for the entire duration of my speech, nearly caused me to forget my closing statement." Her eyes lowered as Ben attempted to interpret her sadness. Most certainly she was recalling the previous version of herself. A version that was on the brink of winning a Nobel Prize for her ground-breaking innovations in science. A version that existed prior to him.

Ben lifted her chin with his fingers, taking in the sorrow in her eyes. "The device you spoke of... that could detect elements via scan...you ever think about revisiting that?"

She laughed under her breath. "Every time I taste your cooking."

"I'm being serious Maggie. I think you should get back into inventing again. You know, maybe just for fun."

She turned and faced the bookshelf, her thoughts quickly displaced by the traces of dust that had accumulated on the books. "I don't know. Why are you bringing this up? Why this sudden fascination with my trace device?"

"Uh..." He rubbed his eyes. "No reason, just thought it might bring you some joy." Think I'll head upstairs and talk to Tristan for a bit and see how he's doing."

As he reached for the door, her confidence bubbled up. "Maybe I'll refresh those patents ... see what inspires me."

Excellent news. Then when he left her for good, she'd have something to hold onto.

* * *

Ben peered into the bedroom where Tristan sat upright on his bed staring at his phone. Despite his sadness, everything seemed neat and tidy in its place. Folded clothes ironed and put away in the closet. Wooden desk dusted with only a single white candle on it, and soft music playing from the speakers on his computer. Hesitant to interfere with the serenity Tristan had confined himself in, Ben crept into the doorway and waited. Tristan's head remained lowered, as he slowly scrolled through pictures on his phone, albeit he knew that Ben was there.

"Mind if I come in?"

He briefly looked up and shrugged. "Sure."

"You coming down for dinner? Your mom cooked pot roast."

His fingers quickly tapped around the screen and a small smile crept upon his face. Ben walked closer, asking, "What are you doing?"

"Talking to a friend," he said, quickly tapping away from the familiar face.

"Through pictures?" Ben hovered over his shoulder trying to get a better look.

"It's an app." He flipped his phone around. "See, this is my page."

"And people communicate with you through that?"

"Mmm hmm."

"May I ask who has lifted your spirits? Clearly it isn't your mother or I?"

He returned his focus to the screen. "Commiserating with Kyle's girlfriend."

Ben squinted. "And that number there, 15,895?"

"That's how many people follow me."

"That many people find you interesting?"

Tristan rolled his eyes. "Guess so... and if you had a page, you'd have two followers, mom and probably me."

"You don't think my life is interesting huh?" Ben joked.

"Not really." He returned to his messages.

"Well, I might just surprise you," Ben humored him. "How do I set up a page?"

"Give me that." Tristan grabbed the phone from Ben's hand. "Probably a waste of time, but if you really want one, we're going to have to pick a profile picture and a screen name. Hmmm how about Tobacco Ben?"

"No."

"Cig Man?"

"No."

"Grumpy Grower?"

Ben shrugged. "That one isn't too bad."

"Okay, now let's find a profile picture. How about this one here of you and mom?"

He nodded.

"Alright, just a few more things, and there, you officially have a page. Wait... whoops," he said, grimacing. "Well now you're Frumpy Grower. It doesn't matter." Tristan handed back the phone. "Not like anyone's really going to see it anyway, except Kyle's girlfriend, she'll think this is hilarious."

Ben tucked it back in his pocket and headed for the door. "Look, I know you aren't hungry, but you should at least try to eat something. No one knows why things like this happen, but they do. All you can do now is be strong and take care of yourself. That includes eating."

Finally sensing some genuine kindness, Tristan looked up from his phone and smiled. "Be down in a few."

CHAPTER 20

Fortitude

Luther sat in his car on the side of the road, mulling over data as the rain poured down. He opened the file he'd been carrying around with him since the start of the case, as if some unseen clue might finally reveal itself. He slid his hand in the folder and carefully pulled out three pictures provided by Kyle McGinnis's grandparents. The first showed him atop a mountain proudly pointing to the elevation sign. The second, his graduation from high school, and the third of him with his two best friends.

"Well I'll be damned." He held the photo up to the light as a message popped up on the MDT. He squinted at the screen, reading the text, "Car 57, we've got a possible 10-80 with a semi-truck at Highway 2 and Steven's Pass."

He quickly typed, "Car 57, copy. En route."

The further he travelled outside the city the fewer cars he saw, making it easy to spot the large rig pulled halfway off the road. Smoke poured from the engine as he ran towards the truck and yanked on the handle. He tapped the window, and called to the empty cabin, "Hello?"

"Over here?" A troubled voice called from the cornfield. The rain beat down as he raised a flashlight into the darkness.

"Are you alright?" he yelled into the towering stalks as a faint voice replied, "I'm hurt. Please, help me."

Luther scanned the field seeing no signs of movement. "Where are you? I can barely hear you over the raaa—"

Pain exploded in the back of his head. Then the world went dark.

* * *

He blinked and the pain hit him all at once, as things slowly came into focus, first the corn stalks then the boots. '*Whose boots?* He looked up to the stranger dragging him by the feet. The man released his ankles, like a bratty teenager not getting their way, as the phone rang. "Bout time you called me."

The pain in his head caused the rest of the words to be slurred as he struggled to make out what the man was saying.

"What do you mean you don't care? Fine, I'll just put him wherever, and *you* can find him."

He paced the muddy cornfield as Luther wiggled a knife loose from the cuff of his jacket and freed his hands. He eyed every inch of the potbellied man, committing his appearance to memory... about 5'5, handlebar mustache, and what appeared to be a scorpion tattooed on his forearm.

Their arguing ceased as Luther put his head back on the ground and closed his eyes. The man paused and looked over the body sensing something was off. "Hmm, I swore I tied your wrists," he said, moving back to the place he had stopped as Luther lunged forward, stabbing him first in the chest then in the throat. He tackled the gasping man to the ground, binding his arms and shoving his face in the mud.

"You think you gon' do to me what you did to Kyle McGinnis? Huh?"

Gurgled words escaped the man's lips as Luther pulled him up by his hair, "You got something to say? Who do you work for?"

He gasped for air, coughing blood as he wheezed, "follow..."

Luther gripped his hair tighter in his fist. "Follow what?"

Eyelids drifted to a close as Luther screamed, "Follow what?"

"The money."

Luther rose to his feet, wiped the mud from his eyes and scanned the miles of farmland for any sign of life. Tears mixed with the rain as he headed towards the sound of the highway, where two headlights emerged in the distance. He limped into the street and waved down the approaching car.

"Officer, are you okay?" a woman called from a familiar rusted Trans Am.

"Linda?" He cupped his hand over his eyes to shield them from the bright headlights, squinting towards the vehicle as the woman hurried to tuck away what bottles she could.

"Man, am I glad to see you," he said, trying to put her at ease. "Listen, I need you to give me a ride back to my patrol car okay?"

She leaned over and unlocked the door. "Happy to help a ... oh my goodness Luther, what the hell happened to you? You're bleeding. Wait... are you bleeding?" she scanned his body for signs of injury. "Whose blood is that?" She looked out to the field then back his way.

"I'm okay. Right now, I just need to get back to my car. Can you do that for me?"

She nodded. "Which way?" When he couldn't answer, she added, "Right now we're on mile marker 6 near the Flowers' Farm."

"We're all the way near the Flowers' Farm? I left my car near Steven's Pass."

"You're a long way from there."

"I know." Attempting to sound neutral as he mulled over the reasons that man had to bring him here, he asked, "Linda, what are you doing all the way out here?"

Her shaking fingers gripped the steering wheel a little tighter as she confessed, "Something happened to all the machines at work... like a hack of some kind. I was supposed to be backing them up every night on tapes, and I kind of forgot. I drove back in to try to see if I could make it right, and," she shrugged as if a thirty-five-year career hadn't just ended.... "they let me go."

CHAPTER 21

Knave of Wands

—·◦·—

Andi shuffled across the floor in an oversized robe that afforded some protection against the chill of her drafty apartment. She aimed towards the kitchen to get more coffee then returned to the mountain of blankets on her bed. A knock came at the door, startling her upright as she whipped her head towards Jake. "Someone's at the door. Stay back here and be quiet, okay?"

Jake disappeared beneath the comforter, his flirtatious words hushed by heaps of material. "I'll be right here."

She wiped the joy from her face and peered out the cracked door. "Officer?"

"Andi Stephens?"

She stared at his bruised and beaten face before answering, "Yes."

"I'm here regarding the murder investigation of Kyle McGinnis, do you mind if I come in?"

"Murder?" She stepped aside and hurried towards the kitchen. "Can I get you anything? Coffee?"

"No ma'am, thank you," he said, taking a seat at the kitchen table.

Fearful he might catch a hint of Jake's cologne that lingered on her skin, she took her place at the other end.

"I'd ask how you're doing but..." she nodded toward the injuries prominently displayed on his rugged face.

"Yeah... you look how I feel," she laughed.

"You worked with Kyle in the lab is that correct?" Luther asked, taking out a small white notepad.

"Yes, we were interning together."

Luther glanced up, trying to get an honest read of her. "Computer Science degree and a 3.9GPA in Bio Sciences, very impressive. Kyle struggled a bit, but I assume you helped him."

She shrugged. "Where I could."

He peered over her shoulder towards her office, eyeing the multi-screen PCs. "That's a lot of equipment for a college kid. What's that? A Unix server?"

"I like to dabble," she replied, mentally scolding herself for not closing that door too.

"You seem to *dabble* in a lot of things... fine art, engineering, computer code. I'm a bit of a luddite. You know, they rolled out mobile data terminals for our squad cars not too long ago and I thought, why replace the radio? It works just fine."

She remained silent trying to figure out where these ramblings were leading.

"Now, I'm not as savvy as you, Andi, but I do know that someone hacked into my unit the other night. Sent me on a mission I wasn't supposed to come back from. Whoever it was made the hack look like it came from Germany."

"Really?" she asked, trying to keep her expression neutral.

"Mmmm hmm. You know what's even more interesting? I now have similar markings on my back and ankles as Kyle McGinnis. Except I was dragged through the corn field out by the Flower's Farm, and I suspect Kyle was dragged through the woods." He pulled a picture from his jacket and slid it across the table.

Andi eyed the ghost of her former lover. "Where did you get this?"

"This is one of the pictures Kyle's grandparents gave me when we were still optimistic about his whereabouts. Tell me, how long have you been friends with Tristan Flowers?"

Her eyes stayed glued to the photo, weighing her answer in case there was a trap somehow. "I met him through Kyle, they were best friends."

"Mmm hmm." Luther pulled a file from his bag and thumbed through the contents. "Looks like you transferred into this internship at Zamka Tobacco from an Ivy league school on the West Coast. That correct?"

She nodded as a spike of fear stabbed into her heart.

"I also see you moved around quite often in your younger years. Let's see... Germany, Belarus, Spain, Patagonia... all before the age of sixteen."

She attempted to head off the next line of questions, by offering up a bit of information. "My parents were pharmaceutical scientists and conducted research in various places round the world."

"And...I see here ..." he glanced at the printed article, "that there was an accident of some kind?"

The pleasant smile she had plastered on her face flattened into a frown. "An accident? More like someone wanted them dead and succeeded."

Luther flipped back to the file, stopping on a newspaper clipping. "Is that because of the drug they invented,

Vivanerol? Says here that the controversial drug would, quote, revolutionize how and why people smoked."

"They made billions of dollars experimenting with addiction," she snapped, trying to hold onto her rage at the injustice that had been done. "Their drug ruined countless lives and was responsible for more than forty-five suicides in the first year. So, if you want to call what happened to my parents an accident, go ahead, but I think other people might call it something different."

His pen hovered over the paper, then finally scribbled something she couldn't quite make out. "The article says there was an explosion."

"Is that a question?"

Luther's gaze narrowed, and she wondered if he could tell he was trying her patience with this topic. "And yet, you chose to intern at a place that built its empire on addiction?" He yawned. "Sorry, didn't get much sleep last night... I was up doing my homework. Want to know what I found?" He leaned into the table, his eyes wide as a child opening a Christmas present. "An article that places your parents at a pharmaceutical convention in Dallas, Texas standing side by side with none other than Maggie and Ben Flowers."

She looked away with an agitated sigh. "Small world."

"Small world?" he repeated with an arrogant laugh. "See, I don't believe in coincidence, and I think you placed yourself at Zamka for a very specific reason. Maybe to tamper with their products, soil their reputation, shut down the very people who partnered with your parents." He flickered a gaze to the computers again. "So, what happened with Kyle? Did he get too close and find out what you were really up to?" He flipped to another picture making sure she saw the image of the crime scene. "What I can't quite figure out is the meaning of the Queen of Hearts cigarette we found on his body."

"Whoa, whoa, whoa! I didn't kill Kyle." She squinted towards the horrific photo, catching a glimpse of the cigarette she had made. "Those playing card designs came from corporate, or at least that's what Ben told us. Each of us had a binder with a specific design, assigned to us by Ben. Check the tapes, you'll see." She smiled, knowing there was no such footage to be found.

"Do you see how a lot of signs are starting to point your way? Tell me, if I logged on to that machine of yours would I see a VPN to Germany? Or did you use multiple hops, maybe went to Egypt first, then Germany before hacking my patrol car?"

An arrogant laugh slipped under her breath. "Nope."

"Speaking of international travel. Can you tell me why you recently booked two one-way tickets to Romania?"

"I like the cold." She stood. "Now if you don't have any real evidence or something to charge me with, I'll ask you to leave."

As he stood from the table his aching back refreshed his anger. "Is there anything you'd like to tell me before I go?"

She averted her gaze from the picture of Kyle and handed it back to him. "I didn't kill anybody."

"We'll see." He headed for the door. "Good day Miss Stephens."

Andi waited several moments before creeping back down the hall to the bedroom, where she found Jake sitting upright on the bed.

"How much did you hear?" The fact that he was fully dressed with his bag in hand answered for him.

"When were you going to tell me that you knew my dad?" She sat down beside him as he turned away. "Was I just part of your plan Andi?"

"Look, I didn't know you were Ben's son until I bought our flights."

"What flights?" he asked, turning half towards her with a wrinkled brow.

"I figured we could get out of town for a bit. Why do you think I had you get a passport?" She could sense his hesitation. "Look, I know it sucks, but sooner or later you're going to have to accept that maybe Ricky isn't coming back."

He lowered his head, recalling the moment he found the empty duffle bag. Deep down he knew Ricky had crossed him, stolen all the money, and skipped town with Jade, but some part of him still defended his actions. "He does this sometimes... disappears into the shadows to wrestle with his demons, but he always comes back." Andi gave him the same kind of look you would give a puppy chasing its tail and patted him on the leg. "And if he does, you can find him when we come back from our trip."

Jake attempted to latch on to any other reason for staying. "How much tobacco do we have left?"

"It's nearly gone." She slid her hand over his, awaiting the questions that she hoped would come. "See, now is the perfect time for us to go explore."

He looked down at her hand. "And just where are we exploring?"

"It is both a where *and* a what.... I think it's high time we explore your talents and make you into the man you are destined to be," she said with that devilish smile that made him yearn for her lips. He leaned in for a kiss, forgetting all about his questions, then pulled back to ask only one, "Just what does that mean?"

She climbed on top of him, answering between kisses, "All this time you've been doing magic in the subway, when you deserve to be on the stage doing far bigger things."

Jake pulled away once more. "You know, you're the only person that's ever believed in me?"

"That's sad... not for you, for them."

"Do you think I have time to go check into something?" he said, standing and facing her full on. "I just need to go see something for myself."

"Our flight is tomorrow night. So, depending on what it is..."

"I think my mom is still alive," he whispered. "And I think I know where to find her."

Her eyes lit up at the sound of adventure. "Let's go now."

CHAPTER 22

The Lovers

———◆◆◆———

Luther kicked the snow from his boots and rang the doorbell, questioning whether or not he should leave right at the moment Sally opened the door. The smell of warm apple pie radiated from her home but he wasn't deceived; the woman couldn't find her way around a kitchen if there were a map drawn out for her. He looked over her shoulder towards the array of seasonal candles upon the hearth and smiled.

"Hey, you." She opened the door a bit wider as a gust of wind blew open the silk blouse covering her black dress. Luther was quick to lower his eyes as he walked inside, refusing to give her the satisfaction of his notice. "Oh, my goodness, sweetie what happened to your face?" she lifted his chin, and for a moment appeared genuinely concerned.

"It's nothing." Avoiding eye contact, he looked towards a safer place, giving the room a quick once over. *Same rug, different couch, same shit, different blouse.* He smirked.

"See you got a new couch."

"Oh, well, I got this a few years ago. So, I guess it's new to you." She traced her hand along the cushions, then headed for the kitchen. "So..." she waited for him to follow before continuing.

He scanned the desolate kitchen, no signs of fruit or any food of nutritional value... not like he had to look far to see that Sally hadn't changed. Despite the smoky eyeshadow and gobs of contouring makeup he could still see the bags under her eyes, reminding him yet again that she cared more for her job than her own wellbeing.

"Is that it?" Luther nodded towards the knife laying in the center of the kitchen island.

"Yeah." She was careful not to touch it. "The flash drive is in my purse."

"You didn't learn your lesson about leaking stories you aren't supposed to?" Though he thought he was over it, he couldn't resist getting just one jab in.

Sally crossed her arms over her chest and huffed. "You know, I should've known better than to call you. I just knew you couldn't let the old stuff go and for once just do your job."

He took a step back and looked her up and down. "Do *my* job? You're one to talk. I shared things with you in the privacy of the bedroom that were *never* meant to be heard by others.

I should've known better than telling you about those toxicology reports..." He paused and scanned the kitchen. "I guess I should be careful what I say, never know when you might be recording."

She rolled her eyes. "Those reports contained crucial evidence in a case that you obstructed. The world deserved to know that Zamka was responsible for the deaths of those children, so if you want to talk about who did their job, and who didn't, I'll be waiting."

"Was sleeping with me part of your job too, Sally?" He locked his eyes on her, making sure to capture the look on her face.

"You know, Luther. This may come as a shock to you, but I actually *did* like you." She nodded as though she was trying to convince herself. "I shouldn't have leaked that information, but just tell me this one thing and then I'll let it go. How did the bodies all wash up in the same place? The odds of that happening are nearly zero."

Luther looked away, then back, rubbed his forehead and sighed. "You know I can't tell you that, Sally."

"Because you covered that up too? I knew you were dirty." She turned away and reached for the half empty bottle of wine sitting on the counter. As she filled up her glass, he searched for the only words that might make things better.

"Fine... you're right."

She lowered the glass from her lips and spun around to face him. "I am?"

"You're right about it being nearly impossible, and I'll leave it at that." He gave the kitchen a judgmental once-over, wondering if there was anywhere in Sally's house that was safe to talk. "Now, if it's alright with you, I'd like to put the past aside and focus on the present."

She took another sip, delighting in the sweet taste of success. "Come on, you really think I'd be recording in my own kitchen?"

He exhaled, wondering if he'd been too brash. "Why don't you tell me about the images on the thumb drive."

She leaned onto the kitchen island, reminding him of what she looked like bent over, ensuring her curvy hips were on full display. "The first one looked like it was taken from outside of my house and shows us kissing on the front porch. The second shows us at the crime scene when the bodies were being taken from the river. And the third is a picture of us arguing outside of the morgue."

"That all?"

"Well, yeah, that and the giant knife stuck in my front door."

"We're going to need to dust the knife for prints, and..." he paused knowing his next suggestion would either be well received or reminiscent of his previous actions. "I recommend you hold onto that thumb drive for now, okay?"

Sally rolled her eyes. "I see you're still deciding what qualifies as evidence and what doesn't."

He shook his head. "You know what, fine, give it to me."

"Gladly." Her tall black heels clicked against the wood floor as she stormed down the hallway. As she walked away his gaze stuck to her like honey, thick, delicious honey. "Mmm mmm," he muttered under his breath, halfheartedly attempting to focus attention anywhere but on her backside. He hovered over the knife, examining the near perfect handle, razor sharp blade, and sticky residue on the side where she'd clearly removed the tag. He didn't know whether to be mad or take advantage of the moment.

Sally stood in the shadows of the hallway, stripped off all but her black dress, and held out her hand with a come and get it look. "Here you go."

He took his time walking towards her, soaking in every inch of the woman he wished so badly to have again, and slid his hand over hers, savoring the exchange.

"I'll get these, uh," he exhaled looking into her deep blue eyes. "I'll uh..."

She pulled back her hand and gave him a flirtatious smile. "Maybe you're right. I should hold on to these pictures."

Luther smirked. "Okay, but, if you change your mind and want me to come back, just call and I'll come as soon as I can."

With each step he took towards the door, he wondered why she hadn't invited him to stay. Before he could turn around and "creatively" suggest such a thing his phone rang.

He looked at the caller ID, questioning the number, turned back to get one final look at her, and headed out into the snow.

"Officer Cooper."

"Hey, Luther this is Maggie Flowers, do you have a second?" she asked. "I know this is your work phone and I probably shouldn't be calling you, but I found something... alarming."

"It's okay," he said, while walking towards his squad car. "What is it?"

She exhaled. "I found a phone... hidden behind a book in Ben's study."

He slowed his steps as she continued. "I was dusting and it just kind of fell out. I know I shouldn't have looked but I did, and I saw text messages from a number I don't know… and I think he's seeing his ex-wife."

Luther gave a relieved chuckle. "Maggie, Iris died some years ago," he said, irritated that she would think this type of thing qualified as police business. "And while I'm sure you're upset, this hardly warrants a call to the police."

"There's more…," she whispered as though someone could overhear. "There are messages on this phone from someone stating that Ben was behind on his payments, and two pictures… a Queen of Hearts, and the other was of a Jeep that looked an awful lot like Kyle McGinnis'."

Luther thought back to the playing card cigarette found at the scene of the crime. "Maggie where's that phone at now?"

"I put it back in the bookcase this morning. Why?"

"Go see if it's still there," he commanded. "I want you to read me the phone number of the person who sent that text okay?"

"Okay, hold on."

Luther hurried to the privacy of his car, settled behind the steering wheel, and pulled out his notepad.

Minutes later, Maggie breathed into the phone as if she'd run a marathon. "Okay you still there?"

"I'm here. Go ahead."

He jotted down the numbers as she rattled them off, noting the unfamiliar zip code.

"Maggie, I want to thank you for calling me today. I'll be in touch."

"Wait, what about Iris?" she said, almost in a panic. "Do you think you can look into that for me?"

"Um, sure Maggie. I'll see what I can do."

He punched in the numbers and hit send as a vibration came from his glovebox. He opened it and pulled out the phone, still muddy from the final moments with his assailant. He watched his number flash upon the screen as another call came in on his work phone. Quickly he shoved the muddy phone back in the glovebox and picked up.

"Officer Cooper."

"Sir, we have a positive match on the DNA results of your attacker. Probably no shock to you, but he's been in the system before and has a long history of violent criminal activities. I see everything here from robbery to assault. It's a man by the name of Tom Wilson."

"Tom Wilson... as in Iris Wilson's brother?"

"Yes, matched the prints this morning."

CHAPTER 23

The High Priestess

Flurries of snow rained down as they hurried from Andi's apartment out into the street. Jake scanned the road, wondering which car might be hers as she split off and headed for a separate building where a single door gave way to a vacant lobby.

With the flick of a wrist she scanned a token hanging from her key ring, and led him into a private elevator to a floor lined with a mix of luxury cars, SUV's, and motorcycles. He attempted to conceal his excitement as they neared the Aston Martin DB4, a car he had only read about in magazines. She rolled the keys between her fingers, switching her gaze between the classic car and more practical SUV with four-wheel drive, deciding which one to take.

Feeling the weight of Jake's stare, she looked up. "What?"

Jake looked at her as if she had just removed a disguise he'd come to love and revealed a monster underneath.

"Is this your car?" he asked, scanning the pristine body of the emerald green '58 classic. Every inch of her was perfection. Yes, it was certainly a her, something this beautiful had to be.

She scanned the inventory with a smile, "They all are."

He bit his tongue, attempting to contain the angry thought that screamed through his mind. *All this time she had money and she never shared it with me. Why?*

Jake took a breath and said something more composed. "I think I should go."

"What?" she laughed as though he had lost his mind.

"Clearly this... whatever this is... isn't what I thought." His inner demons raged on as he turned away from her and sulked towards the door.

"What are you talking about?" She sighed when he didn't answer. "Okay, fine Jake, I have money. Is that what you wanted to hear? When my parents died, I received enough money to last me several lifetimes. Now, can you please turn around and talk to me like an adult?"

He whipped his head towards her. "Then why did you act like one of us then, huh? Were you bored, or... what was it, Andi?"

He could sense something was off as she studied his expression. Perhaps she had noticed the lines in his face that only surfaced in times of true pain, lines that someone long before her was responsible for. But now, in such a shocking time, they were especially noticeable.

"The people in my life never stick around for long," she answered in a low tone. "I just wanted to make sure you were a good one..."

Jake took a few steps towards her and adjusted the cute, off-center hat on her head. "I'm a good one... and I think you are too. And I'm sorry about your parents. I didn't know."

She sealed his words with a kiss and returned her focus to the lineup of cars. "It's okay, they were never around anyway. I've grown comfortable with being alone; didn't bother me then, doesn't bother me now ... until you came along." She returned her attention to the matter at hand and clicked the alarm to the SUV. "My favorite is the Aston too, but she doesn't do well in the snow. We can't afford to get stuck today, it's too important."

"Today is important, huh?" He disappeared around the side of the car and slid in the passenger seat as she fidgeted with unimportant objects; the purse strap hanging over her coat, then her hair. Clearly buying time as she mulled over something.

She started the ignition, heated the seats, and slid out into the snowy streets of East Durham. Without saying a word, she aimed west, as if she knew where she was headed, mindlessly scanning the radio while coasting through the heavy blanket of snow.

Jake looked over his shoulder out the back window, then forward, then back again with more urgency. "Hey, I think we're going the wrong way."

Without questioning, she pulled over, checked the near empty streets, then popped a U-turn.

Catching his judgement out of the corner of her eye, she giggled, "What? No one is even out here."

"Just don't want you to get a ticket, that's all."

She adjusted the mirror towards her face and pulled a tube of red lipstick from her purse, paying more mind to her lips than the road. Maybe he should have asked to drive.

"So, how do you know where we're going?" She said before smacking her lips together.

He looked out of the window towards the gusts of snow whirling through the street, recalling the elements of his vision... *a pine covered forest, snow covered trail, and a wooden lodge with tall glass windows.*

"It came to me in a vision, almost like recalling a memory that doesn't belong to me. I saw a pine covered forest, which if I remember is east of here."

Her eyes remained forward. "And how long have you been having these visions?"

He thought back to the precise moment he experienced his second sight. *Summer afternoon.*

He was on his bike, riding home from school when he smelled something terrible. A cloud of smoke poured from the field behind his house. He pedaled faster, gripping the handlebars as he raced for home. He had just missed the armored car pulling out of his driveway with his mother on board. She banged on the windows, crying out for help as he ditched his bike and sprinted up the driveway. He threw open the door and screamed, "Dad, where are they taking Mom?" Interrupting his happy parents dancing in the kitchen.

Iris paused mid twirl and looked over his sweaty face. "Jake? What's gotten into you? I'm right here." He rushed past them and headed for the fields, finding them perfectly intact, with no trace of a fire. He looked back towards the house, where his parents stood in the doorway questioning his strange behavior.

"It was right before my mom was taken away."

"I'm sorry." She took hold of his hand. "Can I ask what happened to her?"

He was quick to answer. "It unfolded just like my vision… I never got to see my mom after that. When I asked my dad where she had been taken, his only answer was, 'somewhere she can get the help she needs.'"

"And by help, I assume he meant mental?" Andi asked. "Why would he think something like that?"

Jake took a deep breath, recalling blissful memories of his mother. "She could walk into a place and know everything that had occurred there throughout history. The voices she heard were spirits, and they shared information with her that no one could possibly know. She wasn't ill, she was gifted." He reached into his pocket and pulled out a clear quartz crystal. "This was hers. She said that it helped her to slow down the voices of the spirits, apparently they talk really fast." He squeezed it in his palm. "I found it on my bed, along with these," he said, pulling a worn deck of cards from his coat pocket.

Andi glanced over. "Cards?"

"Tarot cards. My mom used to read them." He rubbed his thumb over the weathered box. "Whenever I need guidance, or feel like I need help, I find my answers in the cards."

They neared the entrance into the forest as Jake pressed his forehead to the window, looking up towards the tops of the trees. "I think we're headed in the right direction."

Andi navigated the snowy roads as the questions continued. "Who told you she was dead?"

"My dad."

"And, you don't believe it?"

"Never did." His face hardened as he stared out the window. "A long time ago there was a big scandal that involved some missing kids that turned up in the river. The night before my mom was taken, I heard them arguing, which never happened." His eyes narrowed as he recalled the act. "She said something about finding them in our field. And that the bodies had been moved. The families insisted their children worked in our fields, but without proper documentation, they had no way to prove it. They were certain the toxicology reports would show the cause of death as green poisoning, but oddly enough they didn't. It wasn't long after that dad told me my mom had slipped into a coma and died."

Andi gripped the steering wheel in apprehension. "You think it was a cover up?"

"I think my dad is a horrible man and did what he needed to do to keep her from testifying. Though, she still found her way to the stand."

Andi slowed the car as they neared a fork in the road. "Which way?"

He closed his eyes a moment, before saying, "Right. We go right."

The warm glow from Pine Grove Care Center peered through the trees as Jake's eyes lit up with joy. "There. That's it, up ahead."

She pulled into the main lot and put the car in park. Before stepping out she looked to Jake, and asked, "What exactly are you hoping to get from this?"

He slid out of the passenger seat and looked up towards the wooded lodge lined with tall glass windows and replied with the only word that came to mind. "Answers."

They approached the front desk, where an old woman sat, slowly typing while listening to classical music. She looked up, smiled, and said, "Can I help you?"

Jake gripped the ledge of the mahogany desk, attempting to keep his hands from shaking. The feeling that had haunted him for so long became that much stronger. "I'm here to see someone. Uh, Iris Flowers? Is she here?"

The woman adjusted her small-framed glasses and pecked a few keys on the keyboard. "Irrrrrisssss," she drew out the name while searching the screen. "Oh, yes, here... oh wait, no. Sorry, no Iris Flowers here.

"But..." Jake's hands began to sweat as he leaned over the desk, catching a glimpse of her screen. He stepped backwards for a moment, recalling her maiden name. "You know what, I think she might be under her maiden name, Iris Wilson."

The woman gave a few more keystrokes then nodded. "We do have an Iris Wilson here. Fifth floor, room 504. Now, I'm going to need you to sign in and provide one form of identification."

Jake released a breath that he didn't realize he'd been holding as they slid their ID's onto the counter. Andi raised a subtle eyebrow at Jake's counterfeit license as the elderly woman took a sip of tea. She carefully set her cup back down, scanned their IDs, and handed them back to them. "If you give me just a moment, I'll get your guest passes programmed for floor five."

She reached into her desk drawer and pulled out two key cards, swiped them over a device that looked like a grocery store scanner, and slid them over the desk.

"Now, you will need to wear these around your neck at all times. This card will give you access to the fifth floor only.

When you arrive at floor five you will be greeted by a guard, who will show you to Ms. Wilson's room."

A long, red, Oriental rug lined the hall leading to the brass elevator doors at the end. They walked in silence, observing the perfection of every item they passed. Gold framed oil paintings on the wall depicted serenity every fifteen feet, and perfectly positioned between them were polished wooden console tables with white marble tops and vases of flowers upon them.

"This place is nice...Ricky." Andi laughed under her breath as the elevator dinged.

The sound of the bell caused the guard to lower his newspaper, and squint towards their badges. "Who are you here to see?"

Jake stepped forward and took a breath before saying the two words that suddenly made everything seem real. "Iris Wilson."

He looked the newcomers up and down. "Iris doesn't get many visitors these days. Are you friends? Family?"

"Friends," Andi asserted while sliding a 'trust me' look Jake's way.

The guard's disappointment seemed to cancel out the rest of the conversation.

"Something the matter?" Andi prodded.

"Oh, no." He brushed his feelings aside. "It's just that Iris is... a very special person, and, well she just thought that a certain family member was coming to see her this week."

The guard stopped in front of door 504 and knocked three times. "Iris? You have visitors."

They could hear a shuffling of feet from behind the door, as she replied. "Come in."

The guard peered in, then looked back towards Jake and Andi. "Now, you have to understand that Iris has been in a coma for a very long time, and only recently awoke. While she is in good spirits, she still isn't a hundred percent."

They nodded as he opened the door a bit wider, addressing the bright-eyed woman. "Hey you."

"Hi Mike," she said, walking to the window and opening it as far as it would go.

"You've got some visitors here to see you." He opened the door the rest of the way, revealing Jake's face.

She gasped, placing a hand over her heart and her back against the wall. She then closed her eyes, shuffling over to greet him. Her hands frantically stroked his face, shoulders, and chest before her arms wrapped tightly around him.

"Uh, I'll go ahead and leave you here." Mike nodded while inching out the door. "Be back in forty-five minutes."

She waited for the door to close before erupting into tears. "My baby, my sweet, sweet baby. I knew you'd come; I knew it."

"Why don't you sit down, Mom. You're shaking."

The sound of the word 'mom' coming from his lips made Jake tear up as he guided her to the twin sized bed and sat down beside her.

Those blue eyes, so much like his own, darted around the room as if searching for something to calm her nerves. She looked towards the floor and lowered her voice to a whisper. "You wouldn't happen to have a cigarette would you, dear?"

Andi laughed then slapped a hand over her mouth when Jake glared at her. "Sorry, I didn't mean to laugh. It's just... if you knew what has been happening out there, you'd probably laugh too."

Iris angled her gaze around Jake looking towards Andi. "And who is this brown-eyed pretty girl?"

Andi hurried towards the bed, extending her hand with a smile. "Andi Stephens."

Silence lingered as Iris' lips parted and uttered only a sound, "huh."

Andi awkwardly pulled back her hand and shoved it into her pocket. "I'm Jake's friend."

"Nice to meet you Andi." Her gaze shot daggers through the typically confident girl.

"Nice to meet you too," Andi said, taking a hesitant step backwards.

Sensing some odd form of tension, Jake was quick to highlight Andi's accolades. "Andi is an artist, computer genius, and just bought us plane tickets to go skiing at a resort in Romania."

Iris spread on a smile and looked towards Andi, still with a great deal of suspicion in her eyes. "Would you be a doll and fetch a couple cigarettes from Mike? I know I'm not supposed to smoke in here, but every now and again he'll slip me one. I definitely need one right now."

Andi nodded, eager to escape the discomfort of the room.

As soon as the door closed behind her Iris turned to face him; her smile instantly replaced by alarm. "Jake, I want you to know that you don't have to explain to me why you haven't been here, I already know." Her intense blue eyes locked with his. "Now, listen up, and listen closely. The visions you have are a blessing, not a curse, passed down from your great grandmother, and probably several generations before her. It is a gift... never to be abused or misused for any reason, for if you do, it will come back to haunt you, times three." She waggled a finger at him. "Do not let anyone, ever, take advantage of that, do you understand?"

Jake was quick to obey. "Of course."

She put her gaze on the spot that Andi had just vacated. "I sense a great deal of love between you two, but you're so special and I don't want you to do something just to impress a girl."

The door inched back open as Andi reemerged with cigarettes in hand. "Gave me two."

A seemingly normal smile appeared on his mother's face. "Thank you dear, that should last me a while."

Andi flickered a look behind Iris, spotting a chair in the far corner that would allow them some privacy, and took a seat.

Jake was quick to dig in his pockets, pulling out her crystal and the broken-down box of cards.

Iris sat up a bit straighter, as she stared at her long-lost belongings. "You kept them?" She covered her mouth with her hand and began to cry. "I didn't know if you'd get them, and..." Iris sobbed into her hands.

"Every day, by my side, as a reminder of you... but they were so much more than that."

She attempted to hold back more tears but failed. "You learned how to read them?"

"Kind of... not like you, but kind of."

Her gaze narrowed as she sat back on the bed. "Just curious, how *did* you find me?"

"How do you think?" He smirked, before catching a fidgeting Andi in the corner.

"I know we only have forty-five minutes, and I want to make the most of our time. So... what do you want to talk about? The court case, the children, Dad?"

Iris stood, lighting one of the cigarettes as she walked towards the window. "None of that is important now." She crouched down and blew a line of smoke through the crack in the window.

"It's not?" He moved beside her, looking out to the snow-capped forest. Such a peaceful view.

With their backs safely turned to Andi, Iris whispered, "In three weeks, we will experience what is known as the Wolf Moon, a period just after the winter solstice where the days become longer, signifying the triumph of light over darkness." She took another drag and exhaled towards the window.

Clearly, he was missing some key point. "Why are you telling me this?"

"Because, this is the moment when things come full circle, and finally the light can prevail. I know you feel like you never got answers, but trust me, you will."

He nodded, ignoring Andi's bored expression. "Mom, can I ask you something? I just need to know this one thing... if you called the cops the day you found those kids, why did Luther say you didn't?"

The very sound of Luther's name triggered another deep inhale before she answered, "Luther," she closed her eyes as if to recall his face, then suddenly opened them in what seemed a moment of panic. "He's in danger."

"He is?"

She stared out the window as if she were seeing it all unfold before her. "Isn't that something." A small laugh escaped her lips. "The person he turned a blind eye to is the one who will do him in. See Jake, that is why it is important to always do the right thing, every time." She blinked a few times, returning to his question. "He didn't speak the truth because money moved his moral compass."

"But he was a friend of yours," Jake contested. "Don't you want to do anything to help him?"

She savored one more drag while thinking on the matter. "You know, you can do something to help him. You said your friend over there is good with technology... have her set up a camera on the second bridge just before the house. Do it today, before you leave for your trip."

"Uh, I don't know if we'll have time to do that, but we'll try."

She placed a hand on his shoulder and looked deep into his eyes. "If you do, you will right two wrongs."

Three knocks came at the door as Mike peeked back in. "Hey guys, sorry, but visiting time is over."

Iris embraced him one final time as tears returned to her eyes. She whispered in his ear, gripping him so tightly his ribs hurt. "You are my greatest accomplishment. Because of you, it's all been worth it."

"Nice meeting you Mrs. Flowers," Andi called from the doorway.

Iris flinched a smile and replied, "thanks for taking care of my boy." She kissed him on the forehead and sent him on his way.

* * *

Jake walked slightly ahead of Andi as they headed towards the car, making Andi question his suddenly altered demeanor. She hurried to catch up to him, grabbing his hand.

"Hey, you okay?"

He averted his gaze and looked out to the forest. "Yeah, I... I'm just thinking about something my mom said. Do we have time to do one more thing before we head to the airport?"

"If it's going to another hidden place somewhere on the outskirts of town, probably not," she joked.

He opened the door a crack as she walked around to the driver's side. "She said we need to set up a camera, on the rickety bridge by the river. Something about righting two wrongs. Figured you might be able to rig something up..."

She opened the door and slid into the driver's seat. "You know me, I have more gear than I know what to do with." She checked her watch before patting the seat next to her. "You better hurry up; we have a plane to catch."

* * *

As they sat on the runway, Iris' words repeated through his mind, *"Don't abuse your gifts or it will come back to haunt you, times three."*

"You okay?" Andi eyed the sweat accumulating on his forehead and scrunched up her nose. Before he could answer she assured, "Everything is going to be fine. Remember, we talked about how it would work." She put her hand to his cheek and tilted his face her way. "You're a gifted man, and all those years doing tricks on the street was just preparing you for the real thing."

He nodded. "But those were small things... credit cards, wallets, smokes. This seems..."

She gave him a devilish smile. "Bigger?"

He struggled to find the right word. "Riskier?"

"Bigger risk equals bigger reward. I told you, I'll provide a distraction and allow you plenty of time to do your magic."

Questions pummeled through his mind as he leaned in with a whisper, "What kind of distraction?"

CHAPTER 24

The Chariot

Maggie squinted at the clean-cut version of her husband sitting at the opposite end of the table, sizing up his new façade. Face freshly shaven, shirt neatly pressed, and a small hint of cologne lingering in the air, clashing with the aroma of dinner. He stared at his phone with intense eyes, as if it were the very thing he cleaned up for, while the dinner she cooked grew cold.

"Expecting a call?"

"Huh?" he started, realizing there was another person in the room.

She sipped her wine. "You have barely said two words to anyone in this house all day. Everything okay?"

For weeks now, Ben had been sulking around the house, dividing his time between the yard and his office, remaining suspiciously quiet in both. It wasn't abnormal for him to busy himself with projects, but the nature of his new projects seemed out of touch with his usual habits. The first few days after the plant had closed, he disappeared at odd hours, both day and night. Maggie chalked it up to an adjustment in sleeping patterns and left it at that. Shortly after, he began an unusual amount of landscaping, trimming trees, cleaning gutters, and meticulously pressure washing whatever he could. She assumed his new interest in the outward appearance of their home was to compensate for his lack of work, but that didn't explain his recent interest in improving his own looks.

"Everything's fine." He hurried to pick up his fork.

She silently assessed his mannerisms, sensing a lie. "So, you'll be excited to hear that I've reestablished the patents for my old inventions, and was even invited back to my college to speak to the graduating class."

His phone vibrated causing him to rush from his seat. "Excuse me." The vibrations continued as he grumbled from the hall, "Hello?" He pulled the phone from his ear as a message popped up on the screen addressed to Frumpy Grower. Curiously, he tapped the alert, opening a chat window.

"Who is it honey?" Maggie called from the table.

"Uhm." He lingered in the hall while reading the obscure message. "Shame you never saw the *value* in your own son."

A picture popped up below it, linking to a news article from Romania detailing a grand heist involving a set of priceless pocket watches. He closed the article and went back to the chat, attempting to view the profile of the sender. He repeatedly tapped the image of the queen of hearts only to receive the same message, 'this account no longer exists.'

Ben hurried to his office and sat down at the computer, typing the words, 'Romanian heist' in the browser. An article popped up along with a video of what had unfolded earlier that day; an explosion just outside of an iconic castle, and the theft of dozens of priceless watches. He squinted towards the screen reading the headline, 'Royal Watches Stolen,' and clicked on the video to see more.

A shaken woman stood in the grand ballroom of the castle, looking out from an exquisite window towards the winding roads now ablaze. Priceless pieces of art hung on the wall behind her, which oddly was not the focus of today's story. She turned to the reporter, recalling what happened.

"We were on a tour, and our guide was just telling us of the castle's deep and colorful history." She attempted a smile. "I looked forward to coming here all year. After all, within the palace walls are some of the finest examples of European artwork... German stained glass, Murano crystal, Turkish silk, and of course the hand carved spiral staircase. I strayed from the group, walking in what seemed like a trance towards the window where I saw a fire burning at the base of the mountain. Before I could figure out exactly what I was looking at, there was an explosion that shook through the walls and sent us all to our knees. Next thing I knew, the alarms were going off and all of the watches from the horology exhibit were gone."

"Now for those of you who don't know," the reporter interjected. "These are watches that once belonged to the king himself, some solid gold, others inlaid with rubies... priceless timepieces, just vanished." She repositioned back towards the image of the fire, "At this time it is unclear as to what caused the explosion, but what we do know is that clearly this was a planned heist."

* * *

Sirens wailed as Andi and Jake sped off towards the forest; smiles glued to their faces, cheeks flushed with adrenaline. Neither said a word until they lost sight of the fire burning in the rearview and safely entered the seclusion of Bucegi Natural Park, a frigid place Andi had only explored once as a child. Her wild eyes glanced at Jake who seemed abnormally quiet.

"You can wipe the fear off your face now," she said with a devilish smile. "We did it."

She squeezed his cold, limp hand in hers, expecting a reaction. "Hey? Did you hear me? I said we did it. There's nothing to worry about anymore."

Iris' words spun through his head like a record, repeating the consequences of misusing his power. "I just hope it's okay, you know... I told you what my mom said."

She squeezed his hand a bit tighter. "You used your gifts to help others, I don't see how that can be wrong." She smirked. "Besides, what good were those watches doing anyway just sitting there to impress tourists? At least now they'll be put to good use."

"I kind of wish I could be there to see the looks on the kids' faces when heaps of treasure magically appear in the old church." He turned to face her, posing a more serious question. "Why were you so insistent we do this? You put your life on the line to carry out an act you didn't even benefit from."

She looked at him like you would a puppy, tilting her head with that same adoring look. "I did this for you, so that you could finally see that you're worth so much more than card tricks and street magic." She smiled a bit bigger and asked in a playful tone. "So... you never did tell me, how *do* you do it? I've watched you many times, and still can't figure it out."

He raised an eyebrow, and smirked. "The thing about magic is, if you're good at it, no one ever finds out how you did it."

CHAPTER 25

Death

Ben walked the empty floor of the manufacturing plant, dipping into the break room where he typically finished the day in the company of others. His only company now was the lonely Christmas tree standing in the corner, no lights or decorations, just an ugly plastic tree. The florescent lights shining upon it surely made it uglier, which is why Linda usually layered it in gobs of colorful lights, tinsel, and candy canes. He scanned the area; no Linda, no sales clones, no one at all.

For thirty-five years he had done nearly the same thing every day, but something about this solitary moment felt ... freeing. While things hadn't exactly gone as planned, a small part of him still believed that Iris would understand. He reached for the lights and glanced over the room one final time before heading to the parking lot.

The crisp winter air chilled his bones as he climbed onto his bike and headed for the forest. His mind drifted as he crossed the covered bridge, envisioning all the things he would tell Iris when he saw her. Of how he had planned to take down those that had hurt her the most, to make up for all the evil that was done.

He sped towards the second bridge, lingering between the cliffs, as flashing lights halted the happy reunion unfolding in his head. A familiar voice called out from behind. "Ben Flowers, pull the bike over and put your hands in the air."

He squinted towards the mirror and caught a glimpse of Luther's battered face, realizing for the first time why Tom Wilson hadn't responded to any of his texts in the weeks that had passed. He had paid good money to have Luther taken care of, and now it was apparent something had gone wrong. For half a second, he wondered if this were the ghost of Luther, coming back to haunt him. Some part of him wished that it was.

The grey skies of winter unleashed as snow began pouring down. Ben parked his bike, and slowly put his hands in the air as Luther stepped from his vehicle and stalked towards him. "It's over Ben, we got you for all of it... the murder of Kyle McGinnis, the attempted murder of a police officer, and tampering with goods in attempt to harm others."

He took several slow steps towards the bike and stopped a few feet behind it. "Takes a madman to destroy everything he's worked a lifetime to build." As Ben shifted in the saddle

Luther reached for his gun. "Why'd you do it, Ben... annihilate the family business and take the lives of innocent people. Was it all for Iris?"

Ben cringed as Luther shone a light on his darkest secret.

"Oh, yeah, I know about that too. Followed the money... and it took me right to her."

Ben remained seated and called over his shoulder, "I had my reasons."

The gun cocked as Luther neared. "Well, you'll have plenty of time to explain down at the station. Wait 'til everyone finds out it was you..." Luther smiled despite the nearly healed wounds on his face.

Ben slid his hand on the throttle. "No one else knows?"

"Not yet, but they will.... the whole world will."

In a snap moment he accelerated forward, leaving Luther to scramble back to his car. Sirens blared behind as he sped through the forest, devising a plan as he went. As he neared the ice-covered bridge his tires slid beneath him, tipping the bike, and sending him rolling.

Luther's car skidded behind, swerving to miss Ben, but breaking through the rickety sides of the bridge, plummeting to the river below.

Ben dragged himself from the ground, blinking the world back into focus. He pulled his helmet off and looked over the large crack that could have easily been his head, then walked to the edge of the bridge. The frigid water rushed around the quickly sinking car as Ben scanned the wreckage for signs of life.

A shameful tear slid down his cheek, as he uttered a few words.

"You were a good cop, should've have been a better man. Shame things had to end like this, but what can I say, it was written in the cards."

CHAPTER 26

The World

The sun peeked through the lace curtains, warming the face of the blonde woman whose eyes had been trapped by years of slumber. The silhouette of a man came into focus between slow groggy blinks as she muttered, "Who's there?"

"Iris." Ben rushed to her side. "Careful now, you've been through an awful lot."

She instinctively scrambled backwards, pushing herself up in the bed. He ran towards the small kitchen filling a cup of water. "You must be thirsty. Let me get you some water."

Iris eased back onto the pillow, studying the man she swore she'd kill if she ever saw him again. "I'm cold, not thirsty, and how'd you get in here? Where's Mike?"

He hurried around the room, gathering blankets. "Here, is that better?" he asked, tucking them around her legs. "Mike is just outside in the hallway."

She turned her face towards the window. "Draw the curtains and crack the window. I need some fresh air."

Ben pulled back the drapes, revealing the fog laced treetops of the winter forest. "I made sure to put you in the most peaceful place I could find."

Iris looked down at her trembling hands, angered by the immediate reaction he caused, then pulled the blankets up to her chest, finding more comfort in the inanimate object than in his presence. She glanced over his shoulder with an icy glare as apparitions filled the room one by one; teachers, doctors, store clerks, even children surrounded the bed.

"I came as often as I could," Ben said as tears swelled in his eyes. "I always hoped you could hear me."

The apparitions glared at the man responsible for their state and responded in unison, *"Ask him why you are here."*

"Ben," Iris whispered. "Why am I in a hospital bed?"

Though she was fully aware of what he had done to put her there, some part of her wanted to hear him finally take ownership.

He lowered his head in shame. "I don't think we need to talk about this right now. All you need to know is that you're cured and—"

"I insist."

Ben paced the room in his typical fashion, insinuating a good lie was being conjured. "Well, Iris there isn't any easy way to say this but, you had an illness. You heard voices; saw things that simply weren't there. But you're better now."

She scooted back in the bed as more souls filed into the room, surrounding them in silence. Her hands shook beneath the blankets as she recalled their last goodbye, the sight of his cowardly face lowered as those men dragged her from the house.

"Did the crops grow back?"

"What?" he looked shocked that she had remembered.

"After I burned the field, did the crops grow back?" There was a sense of pride in her smile as she watched him squirm.

He sighed. "Uhm, yes, they did."

She glanced at his hand, eying the unfamiliar wedding band. "Why are you here, Ben?"

"Look Iris, I knew the day I met you that you were different. It's part of the reason I fell in love with you." He slid his hand over the offensive band as she looked away. "What happened out in the fields... it was a tragic mistake. It changed you, and ignited a madness that I just couldn't contain."

Her eyes widened with each word he spoke. He was blaming this on her? How dare he!

"Some days I'd find you sitting alone conversing with an imaginary audience, and part of me chalked it up to boredom, but then I overheard you talking about a strange list of demands. Shortly after, I came home to find the field set ablaze." Even after all these years he still failed to acknowledge the dead children she had found out there, and the coverup that he knowingly took part in. That cursed field.

Iris looked towards the heavily bolted door. "That's the problem Ben, since the day you met me you didn't take me seriously." She stared straight ahead, over his shoulder, to the room of pensive glares, locking eyes with the children. "And those poor children... if you were any form of a good man you would have turned Sam in for putting kids in the field."

"I ... I didn't know he had sourced the labor like that, I didn't know Iris." He attempted to grab her hands.

She pulled away.

"But listen... I made things right... I fixed things. Now, Sam and all of the others who mirrored his actions are going to be out of work for a very long time. Zamka Tobacco is ruined.

She absorbed the derision of the onlooking audience. "And the voices, the ones I told you about, how is it that you've solved that problem?"

Ben laughed. "Well you don't seem to be hearing voices anymore, so I assume all of the shock therapy worked."

She rubbed her violated temples. "You've only made it worse Ben." Perspiration beaded across her forehead as the agitated group inched closer to the bed. "Ben, what have you done?"

He dropped to his knees, looking up with eyes full of pity. "I did what needed to be done to put Sam away, and get people to stop smoking. I did this for you, don't you see?"

One of the more prominent voices in the room offered the information Ben insisted on keeping to himself. "Poison. Framed Sam. Many dead."

Before he could fire off another excuse, the sound of heavy boots surged down the halls. A blaring voice came from the other side of the door. "Ben Flowers, this is the police. Come out with your hands up."

His eyes widened with fright, wondering what more could go wrong. "Ben Flowers. You are being charged for the murder of Officer Luther Cooper, now come out with your hands up."

Iris smiled, thankful that Jake had heeded her warning. "Two wrongs..." she whispered, reaching for the cigarette on the nightstand. Ben seemed more worried about Iris smoking than the fleet of law enforcement moving in as he implored, "Come on Iris, this is how the *old* you would handle stress. The new you doesn't need to smoke anymore." He paced to the window, looking out to the armory of vehicles below.

"You wouldn't understand. I just need this right now." She placed the cigarette to her lips and struck the match.

"Remember our first date? You with your red lipstick and matching coat, you said nearly the same thing," he continued as if the world around him wasn't burning.

Tears filled her eyes as an intimidating figure filled the doorway with his gun drawn. "You didn't believe me then either..."

She drew it to her lips, savoring the sweet taste of relief as a visual appeared before her, of their field engulfed in rays of golden sunshine. Joyful expressions gleaned from the children's faces, and as they reached for her hand the cigarette fell to the floor.

Epilogue

"Hi stranger." A peppy, over-medicated girl with a face free from sorrow said while sitting down beside him. She was the only person in this God forsaken place that he could stomach a conversation with. Though conversations were often repeated due to her fleeting memory, it oddly reminded him of Linda.

Ben returned his attention to the paper, falling into their typical banter. "You shouldn't talk to strangers."

He mouthed the words as she said them. "We're all strangers until we say hello." He could feel her toothy grin hovering over his shoulder, looking at their only connection to the outside world.

He scowled at the vanilla façade of her existence, somewhat jealous of her lack of memories. He could tell everything he needed to know about her with just one glance. Her tired eyes a telltale sign of the trauma she had seen, and the stiffness of her face an attempt to mask it all. He wondered what she had done to end up in a place like this; whatever it was had been buried away deep in her psyche by years of medication. Sometimes he'd poke around and see what holes he might place in the layers of her mind, almost always coming up with nothing.

"Hey Nicole," he turned to face the peppy girl wondering if she would even be able to process what he might ask next. "Have you ever stared into the depth of your eyes?" He didn't wait for her to answer. "You should try it sometime... see how you feel about what looks back at you. I always look away after a few seconds, as if I've accidently made eye contact with a beast that has been searching thousands of years to find me. Deep down, I know it is the truth staring back at me, just waiting for a moment to resurface."

Ben thought back to those final moments with Iris, and all the mistakes leading up to it. The months that followed his arrest had been tricky. Mysterious footage appeared of what happened on the bridge that day with Luther, which was later dismissed as an accident. Detailed information made its way to prime-time news; seems Sally Childs had recorded a private conversation between herself and Luther and aired that information for the world to hear. That was just the story she needed to finally get out of East Durham.

Poisoned cigarettes emerged in Sam Stockton's office, as well as confirmed fingerprints that linked Sam's wife Gina Stockton to the murder of Scott Daniels. Sam took the fall for sourcing the illegal labor, poisoning his own product, and a laundry list of other crimes that came to light during the investigation. Though, he didn't go down alone. Sam was indicted, along with Pete Tooney, and several other high-profile executives. Following the exodus, the stock of Zamka Tobacco had fallen so low that when the time came for someone to buy the remaining shares, only one stepped forward. Maggie Flowers, now the sole owner of the company, had capitalized on selling a device that would test all cigarettes for poison with one simple scan.

The sad, jobless, lonely future that Jake had mentioned in the subway, was now Ben's reality. When he attempted to justify what had taken place on his farm with tales of spirits and cursed land, Maggie had him committed to the very same place he had confined Iris to.

"I ... I'll have to try that," Nicole sprang from the couch and began her hunt to find a mirror.

He returned his eyes to the paper as the phone sitting on the end table rang. He scanned the room of numb minded blanks and headed towards the phone, looking over his shoulder for any sign of intruding staff.

"Hello?" he answered, shocked at the moment he was experiencing.

The heavy breathing on the other end proceeded an excited, rattling voice. "Have you seen the news?

"Who is this?" Ben shielded his mouth and scanned the room with apprehension.

The man's child-like giggle overshadowed any level of maturity his voice had held. "An inspired fan."

He growled into the phone, "How did you get this number?"

"I have access to many things... I'm a scientist... like you."

Lured by the semblance of a normal conversation, Ben asked, "Have you invented anything I've heard of?"

He laughed full out this time, and it sent a chill down Ben's spine. "You're about to... the whole world is about to."

"Tell me more..." Ben quipped, sensing the man was about to disconnect.

"A magician never shows his cards, BUT I'll give you a hint. You never know when danger might *stick* its *neck* out."

Ben tilted his head, looking at an approaching nurse eyeing him with suspicion. "Is that some kind of a threat?"

The stranger's shaky voice deepened. "It's a warning." Screams erupted in the distance as he whispered, "Seems people here are starting to get my *point*... gotta go."

Ben slammed the phone back on the receiver as Nicole plopped down on the couch. "Hi stranger."

He continued thumbing through the paper, scanning past an article about mysterious heists, stopping at the bold reminder of what he'd given up. *'Local Woman, Maggie Flowers, wins Yuri Milner Breakthrough Award and Three Million Dollar Prize.'* He glared at the pixelated faces smiling back at him. Beside her stood their son Tristan, now part owner in Zamka Tobacco and the marketing enthusiast behind her latest breakthrough. With his help, they manufactured and distributed an element detector that could uncover traces of poison with one simple scan. The final nail in Ben's coffin was her newest invention utilizing heat sensitive ink. Her new line of cigarettes was designed to empower women, and had key phrases appear on the paper when lit, like 'you're enough.'

"She wouldn't be there if it weren't for me," Ben grumbled under his breath while flipping to the next page. "Well look at that, finally some good news," he smiled for the first time in days. *'New Bridge Erected in Officer's Name.'*

References:

https://www.opencolleges.edu.au/informed/features/30-tricks-for-capturing-students-attention/

https://truthinitiative.org/research-resources/emerging-tobacco-products/e-cigarettes-facts-stats-and-regulations